IT CAME UPON A MIDNIGHT CLEAR

To: Sue

Enjoy the Ride!

D.M. Gregg
08/11/08

IT CAME UPON A MIDNIGHT CLEAR

D.M. GREGG

TATE PUBLISHING & *Enterprises*

It Came Upon a Midnight Clear

This title is also available as a Tate Out Loud product. Visit www.tatepublishing.com for more information.

Published by Tate Publishing & Enterprises, LLC
127 E. Trade Center Terrace | Mustang, Oklahoma 73064 USA
1.888.361.9473 | www.tatepublishing.com

Tate Publishing is committed to excellence in the publishing industry. The company reflects the philosophy established by the founders, based on Psalm 68:11,
"The Lord gave the word and great was the company of those who published it."

Cover design by Kandi Evans
Interior design by Nathan Harmony

Published in the United States of America

ISBN: 978-1-60604-521-3
1. Fiction 2. Science Fiction - Adventure
08.07.11

Dedication

This book is dedicated to my Heavenly Father who through him has inspired these words in the fight of good against evil. This book was written for the purpose of helping our young people to search and find their higher power to assist them in making decisions between right and wrong. I want to thank my family and friends for their encouraging words and endless support.

Cast of Characters

Midnight–The Cat–a five week old black kitten, which Thomas finds abandoned in a garbage dumpster on a cold winter night. He takes in this little bit of trouble and his life changes, but, he hasn't any regrets.

Thomas Sheffield–Cat's Humanoid, which is what cats call humans, and the lab assistant to the professor. He leaves Missouri to find himself and finds instead the girl of his dreams. His loyalty to the professor is rewarding but it almost cost him the life of the woman he loves.

Professor ReMax–A renowned scientist known for his work in genetics when he successfully cloned some of God's creatures back in the seventies. A bit of an eccentric and recluse, but rich enough to not have to worry about what the world or the people in it think. His life is his work and he is dedicated to producing the perfect genetic specimen, flawless and magnificent. But, his destiny changes.

Telesa Roberts–She was born and raised in Chiptaw, Virginia. A hometown girl satisfied with who she was, who knew what she wanted, and she wanted the lab assistant of the professor. However, she is tested in a way she never dreamed possible.

Papa and Mama DellaVecchia–They came from Italy and settled in Chiptaw where their dream to open their own restaurant came true. Papa and Mama's Italian Ristorante, they offered more than just great food.

Jonathan ReMax–Son of the professor with a successful law practice in New York. He understood dedication and devotion to one's career which landed him in a divorce after seventeen years of marriage. He suffers with early signs of Parkinson's which his mother, Louise died from twenty years ago. He was about to lose the very thing he valued most. But, he receives a generous gift and learns an important lesson.

Tasha Marie Winsfield–Daughter of the professor who married her high school sweetheart. She was the Belle of Society, one of Boston's elite. But, she has much to learn about life and unconditional love.

Anthony Spencer–A seasoned con-artist. His specialty "the perfect sting." He has stolen thousands of dollars from unsuspecting patrons. He gains their trust and then steals them blind. He develops a devious plan to set-up the professor in an effort to steal a fortune.

Bruno DellaVecchia–Son of Papa and Mama. He's associated with the Italian mob unbeknownst to his parents. He could make problems disappear with the help of a little cement and a deep river.

Professor Marian Rutherford–The prodigy student of the professor who graduated with a PHD in Phylogenetics from the University of Washington. She explored human cloning. She succeeds where her mentor fails but there is a great price to pay.

Ghost Kitty–The evil white clone of Midnight produced in the lab by Professor Rutherford. His only mission, destroy all humanoids. His destiny changes as he changes, but not until after he harms the innocents.

Roedee Rodent–A cloned mouse with special powers, designed to destroy the evil white cat. He has to decide if he wants to fight evil with good or relinquish his loyalty and fight good using evil as he struggles to find his place in the world. Does he ever find his place?

Mallory Malone–A woman from the wrong side of the tracks who uncovers the greatest secret of all. Does she guard the secret with her life, or reveal the discovery for her own personal gain?

Chapter 1

Chiptaw, Virginia, according to Professor ReMax, had to be one of the most beautiful rural places on earth with its rolling hills and surrounding snow capped mountains. Valley's nestled below which seemed endless. Rivers and streams rich in minerals flowed with boundless energy. This was the perfect place for the professor's lab located midway up Duncan's Mountain. A very discreet, out of the way, place with the small town of Chiptaw lingering below with a population of less than two thousand.

The professor had few friends, probably only one, Thomas, his lab assistant. He had plenty of acquaintances, some of whom wanted only to get their hands on the fortune left to him by his oil baron father. The professor was very cautious about whom he could trust. A widower and a lonely man, he lost himself in his work after his wife died of Parkinson's twenty years ago. Losing her made the dedication to his work even more important. He had to find a way to help others overcome this dreadful disease.

He hadn't seen his son or daughter since the funeral of their mother and he had grandchildren and great grandchildren he had never met. He was a recluse from his own family and the world. He allowed the devotion to his work to separate him from all things that once had meaning and he often wondered if he would ever see them again.

Thomas Sheffield was only twenty-seven when he came to work for the professor and he was the best lab assistant he ever had. He did what he was told and never asked questions and most of all he kept things to himself. The young man's only interest was Telesa Roberts, a hometown girl who rarely traveled any farther than the city. She was happy with who she was, a woman who found true love in the lab assistant of the professor.

Thomas came to Chiptaw three years ago from Missouri. He was the image of handsomeness with his five foot nine lanky frame, dark hair and manicured hair cut and mustache. Being part Cherokee Indian and French had its benefits, giving him well defined cheek bones and an evenly dark tan. For some strange reason he was drawn to this meek little town unknowing that his future was about to dramatically unfold.

It was a cold winter night in January and a major snowstorm just passed through leaving several inches of pure white snow covering the ground. The wind was calm and bitterly cold—just above freezing. As the ice melted it would refreeze leaving the road slippery and wet.

Thomas was finishing up the night at the only Italian restaurant in town, 'Papa & Mama's' where he worked as a night manager. He hadn't been in town very long and it was the only job he could find. Time got away from him and it was just about twelve o'clock. He finished locking up and made his way to the alley where he slipped and fell hitting the ground so hard it knocked the wind right out of him.

He got up, wiped away chunks of ice from his clothes when he heard a piercing cry. He followed the sound to a nearby dumpster. There he saw a weak little black kitten with a splash of white on his head and chest, who was almost frozen. He extended his long muscular arm deep into the dumpster and pulled out the fragile little feline.

As he held the delicate ball of fur that fit perfectly in the palm of his hand he wondered if it would survive the harsh cold. "Well, what do we have here? Look at you and how small you are, you're so cold." The kitten, helpless and unprotected, shook uncontrollably and continued to cry as the big man wrapped him snuggly inside his jacket.

"Who put you in that nasty place and left you all by yourself?" The meows grew stronger and more intense even though the strength of the little kitten was almost gone. "Come on little guy, let's get you inside where it's nice and warm. I'll take you home. There's no reason for both of us to be alone. I think I'll call you *Midnight*," he said as he glanced at his watch striking the stroke of twelve. The kitten responded with a deep loud purr. As he called the kitten by name, the little cat would open and close his eyes and stretch his paws and knead in the air. Thomas knew then he had chosen the proper name. So, off they sauntered into the night.

The next few days were frustrating for both; adjusting to one another was not an easy task. Thomas knew nothing about cats and Midnight knew nothing about humanoids. The cat remembered only the one who took him away from his mother and threw him in the dumpster in the dead of winter and left him to die. Of course, Midnight thought all humanoids were alike. But, he quickly learns Thomas isn't like all humanoids; at least not the way he remembers.

This was the start of a beautiful friendship. The days turned into weeks and weeks into months and the two of them became the best of buddies. They knew each other better than they knew themselves—they bonded. A bond so connected they always seemed to know what the other one was thinking.

Midnight went everywhere with Thomas, even to work. They played and did fun things that kittens loved to do like chasing string and jumping high in the air, coming down on all four paws and then bouncing up and down and all around. Thomas couldn't keep up with the little kitten's energy. It was invigorating. He couldn't understand how such a tiny animal could hold such a special place in his heart. He wasn't a '*cat person,*' at least not until now.

Their day to day ritual was always the same. Since

Thomas worked nights he slept most of the next day. But when the afternoon came, Midnight was quick to raise his favorite person by taking a long running leap off the tall mahogany dresser and landing smack in the middle of his back. Without delay, his master would rise.

"Okay, I've got the message, I'm getting up. Are you hungry, little guy?" A loud meow followed. "And just what would the little gymnast like for breakfast?" Another loud meow followed but this time it sounded like, "*tuna*." Thomas stopped in his tracks and stuttered, "What did you say?" He heard it again, "*tuna*." Either he was hearing things or this was amazing, a cat who could talk? He stood there in disbelief and shook his head saying, "No, that's impossible." Breakfast was served and the incident was soon forgotten.

Spring was coming and the snow was melting, filling the rivers and streams with crisp clear water. Leaves were starting to grow on the hard brittle limbs of the barren trees. Blossoms were blooming, birds were chirping and the brutal cold was finally leaving. It was the earth being reborn, casting a new season of freshness in the air, bringing joy and happiness to the town of Chiptaw.

Thomas arrived at work with Midnight in tow when he received an unusual phone call from whom the town's folk called, 'the crazy professor.' It was Professor ReMax and he wanted to place an order for Fettuccine Alfredo which he insisted be delivered to his lab midway up Duncan's Mountain.

Thomas tried to explain that they didn't offer delivery service but the professor wouldn't listen. "I'll make it worth your while young man. Bring me what I ordered and be quick about it, I'm hungry."

"But, Sir, we don't deliver. You'll have to come by and pick it up. I'll have it ready for you." After much debate and sensing the desperation in the professor's voice, Thomas decided he would make the delivery. Hanging up the phone he asked, "So, why do you call him the crazy professor?"

The chef explained, "He's a kook man, a screwball, a mad scientist who does weird experiments. Stay away from him man; he's crazy but he's rich, very, very rich. Maybe he'll give you a good tip or use you in his next experiment." Laughter filled the kitchen as Thomas shook his head. His interest in the professor peaked as he prepared the dish requested. "So, where's this Duncan's Mountain?" he asked. After getting directions he motioned for his feline friend to come along.

As they drove up the mountain Midnight started with his chanting meow like he usually does, trying to have a conversation with Thomas. "What's wrong with you boy? Do you believe the professor's a kook too?" he laughed. Nuzzled next to him the cat started to purr very loudly. As they rounded the curve they came upon the entrance to ReMax Laboratories. Thomas thought to himself, *Well, what do you know? Why would a lab like this be so far away from the city?*

At that moment he heard the cat say, "*Job*." He stopped the car. "Midnight, I know I heard you say something, now say it again," he begged. There was total silence. No purring, no licking, nothing at all. "Oh, I must be crazy," he said as he eased his foot off the brake pedal and rolled into the driveway.

"Man, this place is huge; he must have some set-up here." Walking towards the front door with his feline friend following in his footsteps he rang the door bell once and again and then a third time. No one answered. He started to feel like he had been the victim of a teen-age prank when the door began to open making an eerie creaking sound.

There before him stood this tiny five foot five frame of an elderly white haired man whom Thomas surmised to be in his early eighties, wearing a gray dingy lab coat and thick black rimmed glasses looking very tired and weary. "Are you Professor ReMax?" he asked. "Yes, I've been waiting for you, come in and bring my dinner, I'm hungry."

He stepped inside and placed the plastic container on a nearby table. "That's fine my boy, here's fifty dollars for your trouble." Thomas stuttered, "But, sir, this is way too much money. The meals only $10.95." The old man laughed and said, "I told you I would make it worth your while. I never eat out, takes too much of my time away from the lab."

The mature gentleman sat down and started eating, savoring the flavor of the home made noodles and cream sauce. Thomas started to place the money in his shirt pocket and then handed it back to the professor. "Sir, I really can't accept this much money, it wouldn't be right." Midnight wrapped his tail around the legs of his master and let out a big "*Meow*."

"Well," proclaimed the professor, "that's quite a beautiful animal you have there. What's his name? You know, I don't get a lot of company up here. I stay pretty much to myself because of my work." Thomas was curious and asked, "What type of work sir, if you don't mind me asking?" Looking scantly over his glasses he glared at the young lad for a moment and replied, "Its top secret. I can't discuss it with anyone."

Being respectful of his privacy Thomas proceeded to introduce his little buddy. "This is Midnight. He's a very special cat." Staring down at the floor to study the cat the old man asked, "What makes him so special?" "I really don't know sir. I just know he's special." The professor explained as he continued chewing the tasty noodles and sauce.

"My boy, you seem like an honest lad and you like cats. That says a lot about your character. This place is too large for me to operate by myself. I can't seem to find the right lab assistant. I need someone who has the knowledge and confidence to be my right hand. Someone I can depend on and confide in, but more importantly someone I can trust."

Thomas' eyes grew large and his heart sank as he realized this may be just what the doctor ordered but, was it in his area of expertise? "Professor, my background is in bioengineering research and human genetics. I have experience in DNA sequencing and DNA hybridization. I moved here, not to long ago, and I've been looking for work in my field. If I can be of any help with your research I would appreciate the opportunity to work with you. I can show you my credentials and I promise you can trust me to keep my mouth shut."

The professor, stunned with the young gent's familiarity with genetics, said without hesitation, "Fine, you're hired. When can you start?" With a surprised look

Thomas eagerly announced, "How about right now?" With a smile, the professor again looked over his black rimmed glasses, this time in anticipation of a new lab assistant and said, "Tomorrow morning at eight o'clock will be soon enough. I'll start you out at ten thousand. Will that be acceptable?"

Thomas raised both eyebrows and asked, "Would that be ten thousand a year, sir?" The professor chuckled, "No, I mean ten thousand a month, one hundred and twenty thousand a year. Is that acceptable?"

He couldn't believe his ears and because he was hesitant with his response the professor added, "Well, is that acceptable or not? You can bring your cat to work with you if you want. In fact, I'll even supply you with room and board provided you'll make yourself available to me in the wee hours should I ever need you. So, do we have a deal?"

Without further delay Thomas replied, "Yes, sir, we do," as he vigorously shook the hand of the professor.

"Fine, fine, then I'll see you both in the morning. Goodnight Thomas. Goodnight Midnight."

Chapter 2

With each day comes the beauty of Mother Nature in all her glory as the sun rises over the mountainous terrain of Duncan's Mountain. The never ending sky with colors of red and orange fade quickly as the morning sun rises leaving behind the freshness of spring. With the birth of dawn comes the morning dew which rests gently upon blades of newly born grass, standing tall and leaning over ever so slightly in the gentle breeze. Birds sing in harmony, chirping with excitement. Springtime made her way back and all of God's creatures thrived and delighted in the delivery of this glorious new season.

Thomas said, "Come on boy, we don't want to be late on our first day." Midnight cried, "*Meow,*" as he jumped in the old Buick and whined, "*Work.*" This time Thomas' ear caught every syllable. He knew what he heard but he stayed calm. During the trip up the mountain there were brief periods of silence as Thomas tried to interact with his little buddy. The captivating cat kept opening and closing his eyes trying to reassure his favorite person of his loyalty. Thomas glanced over and asked, "So, are we going to work?" Listening closely he heard the cat cry, "*Work.*" Thomas kept driving and talking. "Yep, you and I are going to work, are you excited?" Then came a disappointing "*Meow,*" but all was well.

The ride up Duncan's Mountain consisted of several winding roads which were in desperate need of repair. Winter left her mark on the blacktop and the shoulders were deep and dangerous. Thomas concentrated on his driving but he couldn't stop thinking about Midnight's ability to speak. *But how is this possible?* he wondered. *Am I hearing only what I want to hear? Man, I must be losing my mind.*

Upon arrival to the lab, he parked the old Buick and gathered up his belongings. Being a bachelor he traveled light. All at once Midnight dashes out of the car and into the woods. Thomas calls him but he keeps running away like he's chasing something. He ran after him yelling, "Midnight, come back here, we're going to be late," but he lay hidden in the thick brush. "Midnight, where are you?" Afraid his cat may get lost; he searched for as long as he could. Finally, he gave up and went to work.

Ringing the bell, the weather worn door squeaked as it

opened. He entered. "Professor, are you here?" Not getting an answer, he walked down the darkly lit hallway to what he presumed to be the entrance to the lab. He turned the knob and inside he saw one of the most advanced laboratories he had ever seen, a state of the art facility.

"Professor, it's me, Thomas." From behind a smoked glass window the professor emerged wearing a dull white lab coat which matched perfectly with his thinning white hair. "Oh, Thomas, it's you, good morning my boy," he said as he yawned and stretched. "I'm sorry, but I've been working most of the night and I guess I fell asleep. Say, where's that little shadow of yours who's always following you around?"

"I don't know sir. He jumped out of the car and ran in the woods. I called him but he never came back. To tell you the truth, I'm a little worried because he's never wandered off like that before." The professor assured him, "No need for concern my boy, he'll show up. You know how independent cats can be. Let me show you to your quarters so you can get settled and we can get started."

Thomas followed the professor down the darkened hall and noticed an unusual odor. He kept sniffing the air trying to identify the smell. It seemed familiar, yet, very strange. The hallway was damp and cold even though spring was in the air. The lab was modern with all the latest equipment but the house looked centuries old, yet beautiful with its rustic cypress walls and solid oak floors.

Reaching their destination they entered a large suite which was huge compared to the small room he had been renting in the city. As the door flew open there lay Midnight spread across the bed, belly up and paws kneading in the air. "Where have you been and how did you get in here?" shouted Thomas. "Do you have any idea how mad I am at you right now? Don't you ever do that again, do you understand?" he scolded.

Midnight flaunted his eyes and took one last stretch when Thomas heard, "*Home*." Turning to the professor, he asked, "Sir, did you hear that, did you hear Midnight speak?" Raising his eyebrows above his glasses he replied, "My boy, you're just excited, calm down. Everything will be alright. Put away your things and meet me back in the lab. We've got work to do, important work and time is wasting." As the professor left, a bewildered Thomas grabbed and cuddled his little companion scolding him again, still wondering how he got into the house, and especially how he got into this room.

The weeks pass with days turning into endless nights. After a month or so, Thomas felt like time was standing still. It was getting hard to remember his own name, much less how his life used to be before he took this job. He understood how much the professor's work meant to the professor but he was a young man and he needed a break. During their short time together he grew to know his colleague very well and thought he had the trust of this not so trusting man; so he spoke up and made a suggestion.

"Professor, you know sir, we've been working awfully hard lately. Why don't we go into town to Papa and Mama's for dinner tonight? You know how much you love their pasta and well; you deserve a night out on the town. What do you say?" Much to the surprise of the young lab assistant the professor agreed, "Yes, my boy, you are absolutely right. We could both use a good meal and a night out. I'll grab my hat and meet you outside and we'll begin again in the morning."

The trip down Duncan's Mountain was extremely therapeutic for Thomas. Since going to work for the professor, he had given up his social life. But, he couldn't complain; not with the amount of money he was making. Nevertheless, he found it difficult being a recluse like the elderly man sitting in the front seat of his old Buick.

It was about eight o'clock and the darkened sky grew brighter as they drew closer to Chiptaw. The city still looked the same, quiet and quaint. As they arrived at the restaurant, Thomas opened his car door and out ran Midnight anxious to see his old friends. Once inside, he ran towards Papa and Mama who were your typical Italian couple.

Papa was a jovial man with graying temples and an enormous belly which shook when he laughed. Mama was a lovable woman always in high spirits. Her dark hair had just a tint of grey which was barely noticeable. But, Mama, well she was showing her age, but to Papa she was still the same beautiful woman he married forty years ago.

"Hey, Mama, it's-a Midnight. He has-a come to visit," exclaimed Papa. "Oh, Midnight you-a one beautiful boy, come to Mama." Jumping in her arms he purred and rolled his head against hers followed by a stream of meow's. Mama stroked his gangling body as Thomas entered the restaurant with the professor.

"Papa, Mama, it's been a long time. How are you? This is Professor ReMax from Duncan's Mountain."

"Oh no, you look-a tired," said Mama as she hugged him with one arm and held Midnight with the other.

"So, why have-a you stayed away so long," asked Papa. He tried to explain,

"Well, we've been pretty busy, but I'm here now and man, am I hungry."

Leading them to the best table in the house Papa offered, "You get-a whatever you want. It's-a on the house."

The professor said, "Well, that's much appreciated sir, but we couldn't possibly accept."

"Oh, yes-a you can," said Mama "or we will be insulted."

With gratitude, the professor accepted and said, "I certainly wouldn't want to insult you fine people, thank you very much."

From the rear of the restaurant came a young woman with satin black hair, which hung loosely around her shoulders, and skin so unblemished it glowed in the candlelight. Her walk was graceful as her hips swung side to side in a most ladylike manner. She was flawless—the most beautiful woman Thomas had ever seen. His heart started beating fast as the palms of his hands began to sweat. As she came closer he rose from his chair to introduce himself.

"Hello, my name is Thomas Sheffield and this is Professor ReMax." Their eyes met for the very first time and the glance became a stare. Papa quickly intercepted, "Thomas, this is Telesa Roberts. She's-a our new Manager and she has been a big-a help since you left." Extending his right hand to take hers he couldn't stop looking into her sapphire blue eyes. He took her hand and kissed it softly like any French gentleman would and as she looked into his dark brown eyes the attraction between them was instant and very obvious to the others.

The professor grinned and said, “My lab should have so much chemistry.” They laughed and tried to make light of the situation.

“Won’t you join us,” asked Thomas.

“Oh, no I couldn’t, I’m working,” she replied.

“That’s all right,” said Mama. “You sit-a down and have-a dinner with Thomas and the professor,” she insisted while still holding Midnight. “And-a you, little man, will go to the kitchen with-a me for some milk.” Off she headed towards the back with Midnight watching Thomas fade in the distance.

CHAPTER 3

Dinner lasted for what seemed like hours as the worn out professor started falling asleep at the table. It was late and time to leave even though Thomas didn't want to. "Come on professor," he said. "Let's take you home." Helping his friend up, they walked towards the door. Thomas turned to Telesa and asked, "May I call you? I would really like to see you again."

She replied with a smile, "Yes, I would like that," as she scribbled her phone number on a paper napkin.

As they reach the old Buick Thomas gently places the professor in the front seat and looks around for Midnight, who, of course, isn't anywhere around. "Midnight," he called.

"Where are you boy, it's time to go. Come on little buddy, we need to take the professor home." Frustrated, Thomas moans, "Midnight, if you don't come here right now, we're going to leave you." From the back seat the cat jumps to the front, surprising the professor. "Thomas, he's right here, now come on and let's go, I've got work to do."

Climbing in, he picks up the cat, giving him a stern look and tosses him to the rear. He hears, "*meow*," and "*don't*." He turns to the professor and says, "Sir, tell me you just heard Midnight speak." The tired old man twisted around and saw only a beautiful black cat lying quietly on the back seat.

"No, my boy, you know, I think you've been working entirely too hard. Why don't you take tomorrow off and spend some time with that little lady you met this evening? It will do you some good and then maybe you'll quit hearing kitty voices," he laughed.

"Are you sure sir?"

"Yes, go and have some fun. Enjoy yourself."

The drive up Duncan's Mountain was short as Thomas was still running on adrenalin. He'd never met anyone as beautiful as Telesa and he had a cat who could talk. Was he going mad? His life hasn't been the same since rescuing the frozen little kitten that cold wintry night.

It was a wonderful spring day and Thomas had plans to spend it with Telesa and he couldn't wait to see her again. In a hurry to leave, and Midnight following close behind he says, "Hey, little buddy; I don't think you should go with me today. Why don't you stay here and keep an eye on the professor?"

The normally passive cat started to growl and hiss. "What's wrong with you boy?" Getting into the car Thomas heard, "*don't go.*" When he climbed out the cat jumped in and lay on the front seat with a determined look that he wasn't leaving. "All right, all right, I guess if she's going to like me, she's going to have to like you too. Come on, let's go see Telesa." Thomas was so looking forward to seeing this woman again that he totally forgot hearing the cat speak.

During their journey down the mountain, Midnight places his front paws on the dash, looking all around, becoming agitated. There was a loud "*meow*," as if were trying to warn Thomas of some unseen danger. The cat grew more animated. Clearly something was wrong.

"What's a matter boy?" The growling and hissing continued. Suddenly, a large bear lunged out in the road, right into the path of the Buick. Thomas couldn't stop so he swerved left to avoid hitting the bear, and then right to keep from going over the embankment, then left again only to crash into a clump of dense trees. The car came to a sudden stop with the hood smashed inwards and Thomas was knocked unconscious. The huge bear headed directly for them and Midnight was overcome with fear.

"*Wake-up*," said this frightened little voice. "*Wake-up*." But there was no response. Thomas was out like a light. The bear caught sight of them and paced back and forth. The cat kept growling and hissing which only made the bear more curious. Thomas came to and realized what happened, but he didn't see the bear. As he started to get out of the car he heard, "*Stop*!" Thomas looked at his cat and asked, "What did you say?" Again he heard, "*Stop, bear*."

Overjoyed that he really did hear his cat speak he started shouting, "I knew I wasn't crazy, I knew you could talk. How did this happen? When did you know? What a wonderful thing," he babbled as the cat climbed in his lap and placed both paws one on each shoulder. "*Shush*," purred the mystical feline. And quietly they sat for nearly an hour, when the bear finally decided to leave.

"Oh, no, look at my car. What are we going to do, Midnight? It's too far to town, and what if that bear comes back? Listen, you stay here, where you'll be safe and I'll go get help."

As he closed the door he heard the sound of an engine approaching. It was the truck driver who delivered supplies to the lab. Thomas flagged him down and the large truck came to a stop right in front of the crashed car. "Hey, what happened Thomas? Is everything okay?"

"Yeah, but the Buick has seen her last days. Say, can you give us a ride to town so I can get a tow truck?"

"Well, sure, jump in."

"Come on Midnight we've got a ride."

Once arrangements were made to tow in the car, Thomas called Telesa and apologized for being late. After describing what happened she was so shaken she drove to the city to see him. When she arrives, the tow truck pulls in with the old Buick and seeing the extent of damage she cries, "Thomas you're lucky to be alive. Are you all right?"

"Yes, we're fine," he said.

"We?" she asked.

"Let me introduce you to my little buddy, Midnight. I found him in a dumpster behind Papa and Mama's when he was only a few weeks old. Midnight, this is Telesa, say hello." Expecting the slinky cat to actually speak, Thomas motioned with his hand to say something but words were never spoken by this conniving feline.

"Nice to meet you Midnight," she said as she rubbed his soft fluffy coat with one hand and then the other. "Wow, you are so sweet and so handsome." The little purr box responded to the affection with contentment and rolled over on his side so she could pet his belly. Thomas demonstrated how the bear ran out in the road and how he over reacted and just about got them killed.

She looked over at the car and heard a faint voice say, "*Can't fix stupid.*" She turned around and started to laugh. "Thomas, that is so funny. You have some sense of humor." But, he knew he didn't say anything. He looked at Midnight who appeared to be smiling while licking his paws for his morning bath.

They spent the rest of the day together talking, and of course the curious cat was right there in the middle absorbing every little detail. The evening ended with a friendly kiss goodbye, not only for Thomas but for Midnight as well. Both were saddened to depart from Telesa.

After getting a rental car and returning to Duncan's Mountain it had gotten quite late but Thomas was adamant that he and his little buddy were going to have a man to cat talk with '*talk*' being the operative word. So, down the darkly lit hallway they sauntered and upon reaching their quarters they entered and with a graceful leap onto the bed Midnight prepared for a good night's sleep.

"Oh, no you don't," shouted Thomas. "You and I are going to have a little chat, you get what I mean? And just what was the idea of that crack about me being stupid? It's no use trying to hide the fact that you can talk, so come on and say something. Go ahead, I'm waiting." Of course there was no response. Midnight just laid there without a care in the world, totally exhausted from the day's adventures.

Morning came quickly and Thomas was ready to get the day started because the sooner he finished, the sooner he could see Telesa. "Good morning, professor," he said with an overly cheerful attitude.

"Good morning my boy; I can see you had a very pleasant day yesterday based on that big smile on your face," he snickered.

"Yes, sir, we did except for the accident."

"What accident?"

Thomas told him the details and then asked, "Professor, do you believe animals can communicate with humans? I mean, do you think it's possible for an animal to learn our speech and then duplicate it, just like a parrot?"

Concerned over Thomas' obvious obsession about a talking cat he replied, "Thomas, please tell me you don't really believe your cat can talk. I guess it's possible but there's not any scientific basis to support such a theory. But then again my boy, I believe anything is possible." Frustrated, Thomas took a deep breath and went back to work.

With nine o'clock approaching, Midnight entered the

lab and stopped at the door and sat, studying the surroundings. He seemed frightened as he looked around taking in all the sounds and smells. "What's wrong Midnight?" asked Thomas. "You're acting a little weird this morning. You've been in here a hundred times, what's stopping you now?"

The fastidious feline was acting most peculiar. The room was brightly lit and not at all like the rest of the house that was dark and always cold and damp. The lab was warm and cozy, yet Midnight was very cautious about crossing the threshold. Thomas, aware of the unusual odor asks, "Sir, what is that smell? I've noticed it before. It smells like sulfur, but it has some other component I can't make out."

The professor removed his glasses and looked at the young lad. He took off his dingy gray lab coat and replaced it with a clean sterile one. Reaching for another lab coat he handed it to Thomas. "Put this on my boy, and come with me. It's time I show you something but you must keep it our secret." Thomas wondered for a moment if he really wanted to know but out of respect for the professor, he put on the sterile lab coat and followed him.

They entered a huge metal safe that was the size of a small room. The door was twelve inches thick, made of solid steel. The walls were silver and shiny and the narrow entrance was just that, an entrance into a much larger room. As they went inside the professor glanced again at his lab assistant, this time with a look of fear and mistrust.

"Don't worry professor; I will keep your confidence." He shook his head in acknowledgment and opened the second door and then the third. Upon entering the last door,

Thomas was shocked by what he saw. The professor cloned a human being. "Sir, how is this possible? This is unbelievable. Your specimen looks lifelike," he stammered.

"It's as alive as you and me, my boy, but it's missing one important factor."

"What's that sir?"

The discouraged man sighed, lowered his head and said, "A soul; something only God can create." Still staring at what seemed to be a perfect human clone, the shocked lab assistant asked, "What went wrong professor? Say, aren't you worried about the legal ramifications? I mean, you have accomplished the impossible and the world should know, but, if anyone ever found out, you could be ruined."

With great sorrow he replied, "Yes, I know my boy, but I was on the verge of complete success until," he paused and took a deep breath, "the specimen is alive but my mistake rendered it to live in a vegetative state. I don't know when or how, but somewhere along the way something went terribly wrong. I thought by using my own DNA I would be able to map out the genetic variations, but the experiment failed. All functional elements in the human genome sequence were perfect, except for the one resulting in the fragile x-syndrome, a genetic mental deficiency."

Thomas asked, "You used your own DNA?"

With disappointment in his voice the professor replied, "I have used DNA from many sources, but mainly my own." Wanting to comfort his colleague, Thomas tried to reassure him that everything he achieved was a success in itself. The fact that he could actually clone a human being that was living and breathing was genius.

"Sir, I will help you find out what went wrong. I think you should continue. What do you think?" The professor was more than pleased as he felt the confidence he lost return. "Sir, please, tell me about your experiment."

The old man was tired from his years of work and sacrifice but he was determined to not admit defeat. "I have dedicated my life to this project. My family has suffered and I have lost much in regards to seeing my children grow up and have their own families. After my wife died, my work became my life. But, I feel this is my destiny and why God has placed me on this earth and I must finish what I have started, at least to the best of my ability."

He explained, "It all began quite innocently, doing therapeutic cloning in order to provide needed organ transplants or a cure for cancer, all being possible with this new technology. I even researched fertility treatments that would allow parents who were both infertile to have children with at least some of their DNA in their offspring. I then got into reproductive cloning which was found to be very successful but it too had its consequences."

Thomas stood tall next to the fragile old gentleman whom he had grown to respect and love like a father. As he placed his hand on his shoulder to encourage him, the professor received a divine inspiration. He looked up and said with exhilaration, "Thomas, I think I have just figured out the missing link! Come, my boy, let's get to work. You see, the biochemical mutations resulted in lesions stopping the enzymatic pathway. The induced mutations on the molecular level, which I generated through chemical therapy, changed the gene product such that it gained a new and abnormal function."

"This resulted in a dominant negative mutation, which altered the gene product, and that altered the molecular function. Thus, if a point mutation can be reversed by another point mutation, then the nucleotide can be changed back to its original state and the site revision can regain functionality."

"Don't you see my boy, if this revision works, our clone will not only be functional but he will have the ability to feel emotions like love and passion and perhaps maybe, just maybe, possess a soul?" Thomas was happy to assist the professor any way he could as he too shared in his passion to help mankind.

Chapter 4

Months pass, along comes another change of seasons as Thomas spends quality time with Telesa as their undying love grows stronger. The cool brisk air portrays the first signs of fall. Leaves start changing, bursting into a landscape of colors, brown, yellow, and red as Mother Nature cast her exquisiteness and awe over the mountains and valleys.

Thomas often wondered if they should continue with the experiments knowing the cost of the consequences, but he remained loyal. Not even the love of his life knew what was going on, yet. She accepted the fact that Thomas was committed to helping the professor and she seemed to understand. At least he thought she understood.

Evening came and he headed down Duncan's Mountain with Midnight in tow. They were going to see Telesa and looking forward to their visit. They enjoyed the ride in Thomas' brand new candy apple red Ford Mustang. It sure beat riding around in that old Buick.

Over the preceding months, Thomas spent a lot of time trying to converse with Midnight but the stubborn feline remained stoic. "Okay, little guy, I guess it's all been in my head, hearing you speak. I guess I'll just give up on getting you to say something. But, it sure would be nice to have a little buddy who can talk. Do you know you're my little buddy?"

Thomas looked away, and heard, "*meow*" and "*love Telesa.*" Arriving at her apartment he parked, got out of the car, as the cat ran to the last door on the right. Placing his paws strategically on the wooden frame, he scratched his previous notches deeper and wider. Telesa let him in, he dashed to the kitchen where a dish of warm milk was waiting.

"Hello, stranger, how are you, long time, no see," she said with a look of warmth on her face and agitation in her voice. An exhausted Thomas responded with a kiss.

"Hi, honey, I've missed you too. I'm sorry its been so long, but I know you understand how important it is that I help the professor." She looked upset so he asked, "You do understand, don't you?"

She shook her head, turned and walked away. He followed, finding her in the kitchen holding Midnight and crying—her tears soaked his fur. As he came closer, the cat started to growl and hiss followed by a loud, "*you fool.*" Telesa stared at Midnight and then at Thomas. "You heard it too, didn't you? Tell me you heard it," he pleaded. She looked again at the cat sitting in her lap grooming his self, acting as if nothing happened.

"I heard him call you 'a fool' and he's right. You are a fool to spend all your time with the professor. Can that job take the place of a woman's love who cherishes you with all her heart? I just want to know what's going on and why that lab is more important to you than I am," she blurted as she placed her arms across her chest and continued to sulk. He smiled, pulled her close and held her. She wanted to fight. She was angry and she wasn't about to give in, but slowly she succumbs to his loving embrace as they snuggle in front of the fire.

Midnight tried to climb between them when Thomas said, "Oh, no you don't little man. You're going outside for a while, we need to be alone." He took the cat by the scruff of the neck and tossed him gently out the door when he heard, "*Bully.*" However, this special moment was not going to be interrupted by a talking cat.

As the hour grew late, their earlier conversation continued. "So, Thomas, dear, as I was saying, why is the professor's work more important to you than I am?"

With a look of uncertainty he took time to think before he spoke, "Telesa, I love you with all my heart and I know you love me. I know God has meant for us to be together for the rest of our lives. I need you to understand how important it is to me to help the professor. We are so close to finding the flaw," he paused, "please, just trust me." She started to mellow. "Speaking of earlier," he said, "tell me the truth. Did you hear Midnight speak?"

With a strange look she turned to him and laughed, "Are you serious? I knew it was you all the time." There were no words to describe how he felt. He arose from the couch and went to the door to let in the cat.

"Hey, little buddy, come here, we're waiting for you." They heard the sound of paws running across the bare wooden floors as he raced inside, stopping dead in his tracks. "Okay, young man, quit showing off," he said in a gruff voice. Midnight started to growl. He hissed and swatted his paws trying to strike his master. "What's your problem?" asked Thomas. All of a sudden the cat lunged towards him and jumped high in the air like a tiger capturing his prey. Thomas moved and the angry feline crashed into the table.

"Midnight, you're acting really strange. What's gotten into you? Now behave yourself." The cat leaped again, soaring across the room, boiling with rage, hissing and growling, letting it be known that he was one unhappy kitty.

Thinking the big ball of fur needed an attitude adjustment, Thomas stopped in the middle of the room and looked him square in the eye. You could sense the unspoken words being exchanged between them, each one trying to be stronger than the other.

"Stop it you two, before somebody gets hurt," shouted Telesa. "I don't know what this is all about but it has to stop." Midnight continued to growl and hiss and started panting very heavily. He was in obvious distress.

"Thomas, what's wrong with him? He's having problems breathing, do something," she cried. Trying to take hold of the savage little beast wasn't easy and he was scratched and bitten several times before managing to put him in a cardboard box.

All the way up Duncan's Mountain the cat moaned in agony. His growling and hissing was constant. As he arrived, the box grew silent and Thomas noticed that familiar scent.

With haste he grabs the box and runs inside and sees the professor coming out of the lab. "Sir, sir, its Midnight," shouted Thomas who was about to hyperventilate.

"Calm down, my boy, let's take a look." As he opened the box, there lay Midnight barely breathing, the professor also noticed the smell. "Oh, my, this isn't good. Thomas, get him in the decompression chamber quickly or we're going to lose him."

Not understanding what was going on, the distraught lab assistant picked up his little buddy and followed the professor. "Thomas, put him here and go to the control panel and hit buttons two, three, and nine." Doing exactly what he was told he pushed buttons two, three, and nine and waited. The chamber had a sudden flash of light, red, green, and blue.

"Professor, what's happening?" The lights were continuous. First red, then green, and finally blue. Out of the blue light came a brilliant white light, so bright they were forced to look away. "Professor, what's happening?"

"My boy, I need to be certain he gets exposed to the cycle of lights if you want to save him. We have to take action now or it may be too late."

The rotation of lights was steady, followed by a low

pulsating hum, a piercing screech, and a high pitched ring. And just as the professor expected, the entire process came to a halt. The room was quiet. The lights went dim and the odor faded. The anticipation was more than Thomas could bare and he couldn't breathe.

"Calm down, my boy and open the chamber." Consumed with fear he opened the door only to see Midnight sitting there looking better than ever. But, something was different. The white spots on his chest and head were gone, his coat was solid black.

"Midnight are you all right?" he asked. The cat nodded his head, "yes." "Sir, did you see that? Did you see him nod his head and say he was okay?"

"Yes, my boy, now bring him over here and let's have a look."

As the eager scientist turned around, Thomas reached inside the chamber and watched as his cat disappeared and reappeared on the exam table. "Well, that was quick," said the professor.

"But, sir, I didn't move him. He did that all by himself."

Giving him that all too familiar look over his glasses, he proceeded to examine the cat. Placing the stethoscope on his chest he said, "Um, that's interesting. Very, very interesting. Thomas, come here and tell me what you hear."

He placed the stethoscope in his ears and listened. He heard nothing, nothing at all. "Sir, I don't hear anything. There's not a heartbeat but he's alive and breathing. I don't understand. How can that be?"

Midnight sat gallantly on the table looking at the professor and Thomas just as curiously as they were looking at him. "I don't understand it either." Taking a moment to ponder, the professor noticed a small amount of light illuminating from the cat's collar.

On inspection he noticed the collar was seamless and fit perfectly around the neck. It was clear and smoother than any type of material he had ever seen. He tried to remove it but realized a strange force forbid its removal. "Wow," said Thomas. "I've never seen anything so beautiful. Look professor, it's a silver pendant." It was plain and bare with a silvery gloss. Suddenly, right before their eyes, they witnessed the spelling out of the name *Midnight*, one letter at a time with such precision it left the pendant perfect and flawless.

A telepathic message followed. "*It Came Upon A Midnight Clear*, *peace on earth and good will to men*."

"What did you say?" asked the professor.

"I didn't say anything. I thought you said something about Midnight and good will."

For the next few hours they stayed focused on the little creature that came from a near death experience to a supernatural state. It wasn't long before they realized he could communicate with them telepathically. They also discovered he was capable of disappearing and reappearing at will.

Thomas asked, "Can you really understand me little guy? Can you tell us what happened to you?" The collar around his neck glowed as the handsome feline nodded his head and started to purr, but his purr sounded shallow from how Thomas remembered. Gradually, they could hear Midnight's telepathic responses and they listened carefully.

"*This is not my body. The remainder of my nine lives has*

been captured in this body. My soul is lost and I feel a yearning to go home but I have no home. What should I do Thomas? I want to go home."

"Are you in any pain?" asked the professor.

"No, I have only a strong desire to return home."

"Did you hear him Professor?"

"Yes, my boy, I did and it is incredible. I just don't know how this happened."

The cat sent another message. *"I fell into the vat of chemicals. I didn't intend to, I was just being curious. After all I am a cat."* They chuckled.

"Professor, do you know what this means? It means your experiment works. Midnight is in the body of his clone and he is functional. Don't you see sir; you have succeeded in doing something that no one else in the world has done."

Looking troubled he said, "But, I don't know how to duplicate the process. Midnight, tell me about this desire you're feeling to return home. And you say you have no soul?" Their communicating back and forth, lasted most of the night. "We better get some rest," suggested the professor. Thomas and his furry little companion took their usual stroll down the dark hallway. The corridor lit up each time the cat sent a telepathic message. Upon reaching their quarters they collapsed and fell into bed sleeping the rest of the night.

Chapter 5

When morning came, Thomas woke only to discover Midnight gone. He and the professor searched everywhere and couldn't find him. The phone rang and Thomas answered, "Hello, ReMax Laboratories here."

"Darling, is that you," asked Telesa.

"Yes, honey, I'm sorry I didn't call you, but so much has happened since last night." The professor stood next to his frazzled lab assistant motioning him to keep quiet.

"Thomas, is Midnight there with you? There's a cat here that looks just like him but he's somehow different. When I got up this morning he was laying in bed next to me." "Yes, honey, it is Midnight. Take him to the door and let him out, he'll come home." "But, it's so far up Duncan's Mountain, he might get hurt."

"Okay, then I'll come and get him." Hanging up the phone he dashed out the door and arrived shortly after at Telesa's. Upon entering her apartment he observed the enchanting kitty sitting on her lap after having finished off a warm bowl of milk. He and his little buddy were able to communicate telepathically and Midnight understood he could not tell anyone about the professor's work, not even Telesa. Thomas also informed him how some crazy scientist would love to get their hands on him and dissect him just to see what makes him tick. Midnight understood completely and agreed a cloned body was better than no body at all.

Kissing Telesa goodbye they departed and headed up the mountain. As they drove, they conversed telepathically. Midnight asked about the professor's family and wondered why he lost contact with his children. Thomas divulged that he chose to dedicate his life to science. Unfortunately his relationship with his family suffered and he often wondered if he would live long enough to see them before he dies.

Midnight, with a saddened look, turned to Thomas and said, "*The professor is going to die and very soon. We must reconnect him with his family.*"

Thomas, in disbelief asked, "How do you know he's going to die? Only God knows." With a loud purr the cat conveyed, "*I don't know when or how, only that the time is near. I'm being guided by an unknown force, to find his family and reunite them before it's too late."*

Thomas asked, "Does he know?"

"He knows he has little time to complete his work. But, he has to change his focus to himself and not his work. See what you can do to help him until I get back." The mysterious black cat faded away.

Many days pass as do several attempts to get the professor to take some time off. Finally, he agrees and they enjoy the splendor of a beautiful fall day by having a picnic with Telesa. "Oh, my," said the professor, "I haven't seen an autumn day like this in a long time. This was a good idea. Thank you for inviting me." The leaves were at their peak with shades of gold and red creating a canopy of color glistening in the afternoon sun. The temperature was a comfortable seventy degrees and the wind blew ever so gently, sweeping across the fields and valleys. The mountain streams carried the flow of rushing water, which was abundantly clear. You could smell the crisp air, which radiated with the scent of spruce pines. However, the refreshing breeze was disrupted by the smell of smoke, followed by an enormous explosion.

Flames shot high in the air. The blaze was an inferno of combustible chemicals, which detonated one after the other, leaving a trace of its contents loose in the atmosphere. At once the professor knew it was the lab. His life's work was going up in smoke and there wasn't anything he could do but stand there and watch in horror as the fire trucks and firemen tried to douse the flames. As the old house burned ferociously to the ground he prayed the lab underground would be spared. He couldn't risk telling the authorities about its location or his work would be discovered.

The fragile white-haired man became disoriented and started to faint but Thomas caught him in the nick of time. "Professor, are you all right? Sir, can you hear me? Can we get a paramedic over here? The professor has passed out. Please someone we need help," pleaded the agitated lab assistant.

A medic came to his aid and after checking his vitals gave him smelling salts to revive him. Returning to consciousness the professor shouted, "Save the genomes, save the genomes." The medic asked what he was talking about and Thomas said, "Nothing, he's just an old man who's a little eccentric."

Telesa tried to help calm him, not understanding what he was talking about either. Later, she cornered Thomas and asked him exactly what the professor meant and she wanted a straight answer. "Honey, he was just talking nonsense. Don't worry your pretty little head over the professor. He was just a little incoherent, that's all." Telesa accepted this explanation, at least for now.

"Thomas, where's Midnight?" she asked in a frantic voice.

"He's okay, I have uh, sent him away for a few days." Looking strangely at him, she questioned if he was telling her the truth.

She asked again, "Are you sure he's okay?" With the nod of his head she stopped worrying.

The professor took a suite at the Shady Acres Hotel, located in the city below. Thomas stayed the night trying to console his troubled friend. The next morning they returned to the lab and the firemen had sectioned off the area. Signs were posted, '*Do Not Enter*,' and a hazmat team was called in to assess possible toxic air pollutants. Thomas turned to the professor and asked, "Is there anything they should know about sir?"

"Perhaps, but I don't think the affects will be detrimental. The radioactive waste will be more of a problem than the air pollutants. I need to speak with the hazmat team to assure them there is no danger."

"You can't sir. What if they discover what you've been doing here?" Nevertheless, the professor met with the hazmat team and provided them with as little information as possible in order to gain access to the lab. The hazmat team performed their routine testing and based on negative results, gave the professor clearance to enter.

The fire totally destroyed the old house, leaving little proof that a house ever stood there in the confines of the mountain. Walking carefully amongst the rubble they searched diligently for the entrance to the underground lab. Finally, they found the steel encased vault. It melted from the extreme heat. "Thomas, we must get some cutting torches and see if we can get into the vault. I have to see if the specimen survived," beseeched the professor.

"Yes sir. I'll go into town and get some tools and be right back. You should perhaps come with me."

"No, I'll stay here. Go on and get back as soon as you can."

The faithful lab assistant was gone for over an hour. The professor found a tree stump to sit on while he contemplated. He felt his life was over—everything was lost. All his years of work wasted. He had no reason to live. At that instant he saw a flash of light and from behind the light emerged Midnight.

At first glance the professor thought he was seeing things, only to have the magical feline jump in his lap and begin to purr. "*I'm here professor and I'm safe and so are you. Your life is not over but it has to change.*" About that time Thomas returned with the cutting torch and started cutting away the first steel door, and then the second. Surprisingly the inner layer of steel was intact. As they opened the third door, the contents within were only partially destroyed but the clone had been totally ingested by the flames.

The professor was heartbroken. His despair was more than any one man could endure. All was lost. Midnight, walking in line with the flashlight, noticed the small floor safe and nudged Thomas. "Professor," he shouted. "The safe, it's untouched. Put in the combination." With great anticipation he turned the dial. Two to the left, three to the right, nine to the left and '*click*' the door opened. The files from all his years of research were safe and unharmed. Even the specimen jar containing his DNA samples were preserved. All had not been lost.

CHAPTER 6

Tasha Marie Winsfield was the belle of society in Boston, Massachusetts. She didn't look her age of fifty years. She could be described as a handsome woman with a matronly hourglass shape, which curved in all the right places. Of course she had her grandfather's fortune, as well as her husband's wealth to help keep her looking her best. She married her hometown sweetheart, Steven Winsfield, who became a famous published author of self-help books based on his years of practice as a successful psychologist. Yes, she was Miss Society and she let it be well-known she was the best society had to offer. They have two daughters, Rose Marie and her younger sister, Amanda Renee. Rose Marie was the mother of three year old twins and Amanda Renee was about to reach the tender age of sixteen, and be introduced to society with a debutante ball in her honor. It was going to be a most spectacular social event.

Jonathan Remax, son of the professor, was a successful lawyer practicing criminal law in New York City. He understood dedication and devotion to one's career, which landed him in a divorce after seventeen years of marriage. He suffers with early signs of Parkinson's, which his mother, Louise, died from twenty years ago. His son, Robert, married Lorraine and they have three children, ages nine, ten, and twelve. Jonathan never dreamed that at age fifty-two he would have to give up a thriving law practice because of his failing health. His firm was his life and like his father, he sacrificed his wife and family only to have it taken away from him in the end. Taking after his mother, Jonathan was fair-skinned with light brown hair which just started graying at the temples. He was a tall man, towering over six feet with large hands, muscular arms and a physically fit physique, that would twitch and jerk with involuntary movements. He was dreadfully frustrated about his future, but, nonetheless he took on the challenge with a positive outlook and valued each passing day as a generous gift.

Working late one evening in his high rise office in Manhattan he witnessed a phenomenal event when he was paid a visit by Midnight. "*Meow, meow,*" echoed the sound of this feline soprano. "*Meow, meow,*" which grew louder and louder until finally Jonathan opened the door to see what all the noise was, only to find the satin black cat sitting in the doorway.

"Well, how did you get in here," he asked as he reached down and picked up the bundle of fur. Followed by a vibrating purr, Midnight cooed and looked the life sized man in the eye, sending him a telepathic message. *"Call Tasha, call Tasha,"* which he repeated over and over again. Placing the cat on the floor, he went to the phone and dialed his sister's number, even though they hadn't spoken in over five years.

It rang several times and he was just about to hang up when he heard a faint voice in the distance. "Hello, hello? Is anyone there? Hello?"

Placing the phone back to his ear he asked, "Tasha, is that you? This is Jonathan, how are you?"

Being the prim and proper socialite she was she responded, "Yes, this is Mrs. Winsfield. Who did you say you were?"

"This is your brother, Jonathan."

She blushed, "Oh, for heaven's sake, how are you brother? This is so strange because I was just thinking about you."

They spent the next few minutes trying to catch up, when the cat jumped in Jonathan's lap and relayed another message. *"Your father is dying. You must go see him now."*

The next thing he knew he asked Tasha, "So, have you heard anything from dad since mom died?"

"No, but I've been thinking a lot about him lately and I don't know why. I hardly ever think about him, and why should I? He never cared about us anyway," she blurted with obvious resentment.

"Now, don't be that way Tasha. We haven't exactly stayed in touch either. You know how important Dad's work has always been to him; can't you forgive and forget?"

"I don't know. I've spent a lot of years in therapy because of that man. Why should I forgive him and how could I ever forget?"

There was silence. Jonathan spoke, stuttering his words as he tried to explain, "Tasha, you know, sometimes we do things we later regret. All part of life's lessons, I suppose."

She asked, "So, how is …"

"We're divorced. Seventeen years of marriage down the drain because I thought my career was more important than my family and now," he paused, "it's too late and I can't change the past."

They talked for more than an hour with Midnight pacing back and forth on Jonathan's antique cherry wood desk leaving smudged paw prints everywhere he stepped. He rolled around on a stack of papers causing them to fall on the floor. Distracted by the noise Jonathan asked his sister to hold on. Looking at the mysterious cat he said, "Be careful boy, these are very important papers." As he lifted the receiver he heard a distant voice cry, *"Chiptaw, Virginia."*

"Sorry about that sis but this cat was knocking things off my desk and …" He suddenly felt drained. "That's the strangest thing," he said.

"What?" asked his annoyed sibling.

"Chiptaw, Virginia. Tasha we must go to Chiptaw as soon as possible." She was stunned by his suggestion.

"Why in the world would I want to go to ... where did you say?"

"I can't explain it, but something inside is telling me to go to this place. I think it may have something to do with Dad. Maybe he's in trouble or sick. I don't know how I know, I just know. Will you meet me there?"

She was quick to reply, "Sorry, brother dear, but I'm in the middle of planning Amanda Renee's debutante ball and there's just way too much to do. You know she'll be sixteen next month and I've been looking forward to this social event ever since the day she was born."

He said his goodbyes and looked around, realizing the cat was gone. After spending twenty minutes looking for him, he gave up and grabbed his coat and headed home. He packed a bag and made reservations to fly into Roanoke, which was the closest big city to Chiptaw. Early the next morning he left for the airport and boarded the plane. While in flight, he thought back to the good times he shared with his father. Like when they went fishing and he always managed to catch more fish then his Dad, but who kept count? And the family picnics on those long summer days. But, the fond memories merged with the sad ones and Jonathan tried his best to hold back the pain.

Meanwhile, Tasha was starting her day choosing a caterer for her daughter's aristocratic event. While sitting in the exquisiteness of the beautifully decorated room of red, white, and blue, she spied a large black cat sitting outside on the window sill. The cat was staring directly at her, making her very uncomfortable. She got out of her chair, walked over to the window and pulled down the shade. But, before she could pull the shade all the way down, Midnight sent her a message. *"You awful woman, your father needs you. Go to Chiptaw, Virginia now."* She quickly opens the shade only to find the mysterious cat gone. She felt very peculiar but her years in therapy told her she was just feeling guilty, so she decided to ignore the incident. However, she couldn't and all through the day she kept hearing those words, *"You awful woman, your father needs you. Go to Chiptaw."* After hearing Jonathan make the same suggestion, she speculated and questioned whether there really was something to this strange message. *And where did it come from?* she wondered. Her emotions overpowered her and she caught the next flight to Roanoke. She thought, *I must be crazy leaving behind my high class friends to visit some rural city in Virginia. And I have no idea why I'm even going.*

Jonathan had already arrived, rented a car and found his way to Chiptaw. He was awed by the beauty of the countryside. The weather was absolutely gorgeous with a bit of chill in the air. The wind smelled fresh and clean. The leaves radiated in colors of autumn; vivid tints of red and yellow with shades of brown reflecting in the afternoon sun. The water in the streams trickled over smooth stones, tossing around trout and gushing into the river where the rush of water turned into rapids. This was so much different than the hustle and bustle of Manhattan. How he longed to spend time in this peaceful place.

Making his way to the local diner he entered and made an inquiry, "Excuse me," he said to the saintly woman standing behind the counter with her hair in a bun. "Can you tell me if a Professor ReMax lives in the area?" She studied him for the longest time before she answered.

"Yeah, he used to live up on Duncan's Mountain but he don't live there anymore since the fire."

Troubled, Jonathan asked, "Do you know where I can find him, it's very important?"

She said, "Well, you might try over at the Shady Acres. I heard that's where he's probably stayin.' Say, who are you anyway, and why you got so many questions about that crazy old man?"

With a gruff voice he answered, "I'm his son."

Finding his way to the hotel, he asked the clerk at the front desk if Professor ReMax was a registered guest.

"Well, I can't tell you that sir. It's against the rules, don't you know?" Thomas walked by and overheard the conversation. He cautiously approaches the stranger and introduces himself.

"Hello, sir. I don't mean to intrude but I overheard you inquiring about Professor ReMax. May I ask why you're looking for him? Perhaps I can help."

Jonathan was an excellent lawyer and he knew how to read people and looking Thomas over, he answered, "You might say I've been sent here by his family." Thomas was suspicious and asked, "Well, what does his family want with him? He hasn't seen his children for at least twenty years."

Jonathan realized this man probably knew his father better than he did so he revealed the truth. "Well, actually, I'm the professor's son, Jonathan ReMax." He extended his hand for a friendly handshake. "I know it sounds crazy but this cat showed up in my Manhattan office and told me to come here. Now if you know anything about my father and where he is, it's very important that I see him, as soon as possible." And so enters Midnight and Jonathan exclaims, "That's the cat, right there. Man, I must be losing my mind."

Thomas knew then, he was telling the truth as he motioned to his little buddy and said, "Come on boy let's take Jonathan to see his father."

They took the elevator to the fifth floor and walked down the brightly carpeted hallway to room five-o-one. Thomas knocked on the door. "Professor, it's Thomas and I have a surprise for you. Please open the door." A short time passed and the door opened and there stood a balding white haired man with a small fragile frame and an astonished look on his face. He knew right away it was Jonathan.

"Son, how are you? I'm so glad you're here. Come in, sit down and tell me how you found me after all these years." Tears filled their eyes as they embraced. Midnight jumped on the sofa next to the professor.

"Dad, it's so wonderful to see you. I don't understand it, but I'm here because I was lead here by that cat. I know it sounds crazy but I'm telling you that cat was in my office the day before yesterday." Petting the furry feline, the professor smiled, knowing only to well that what he was saying was true, but how could he explain this to his only son? "Jonathan, that sounds a little ridiculous but, for whatever reason you're here, I couldn't be more delighted."

Shortly after, Tasha arrived in town. She went to the same diner and spoke to the same saintly woman. "Madam, I am looking for a Professor ReMax. Can you tell me where I may find him?"

The woman raised her eyebrows and rolled her head back and whispered to the other waitress, "What is it with that old man? Why is everybody all of a sudden lookin' for him?" She turned to Tasha and asked, "And who might you be missy that I would want to tell you anything about that old kook?"

Tasha was not amused. She may not have had the utmost respect for her father, but she certainly wasn't going to stand around and let anyone else speak ill of him. In a forceful tone she shouted, "Why you low life, good for nothing, vicious woman. It's none of your business who I am. You either know where he is or you don't. I haven't the time or the patience to put up with you, Missy." She spun around and walked towards the door only to hear the reply, "Try the Shady Acres."

The hotel wasn't hard to find in such a small town. In fact it was just up the road nestled below Duncan's Mountain surrounded by the illustrious colors of fall which even Tasha had to stop and take notice. Upon her arrival she inquired about the professor. The same clerk who was on duty earlier grinned and said, "You know, you are the second person today askin' about him. But I can't tell you nothin,' don't you know, 'cause I ain't supposed to." Tasha was not in the best of moods after having to deal with the hair bun lady. So, being her usual forceful self, and used to getting whatever she wanted, she placed a hundred dollar bill in his hand and said, “Now, tell me the room number or this goes back in my purse.”

Having never been bribed with this much money before, it caused the clerks voice to crack. He looked around to see if anyone was watching and whispered, “Room five-o-one,” as he placed the bill in his shirt pocket. As she stomped away she heard him yell, “Oh, by the way, the elevators broken. Just happened, so, if you wanna get up there, you gotta take the stairs.” She was absolutely appalled at having to walk up five flights of stairs. She was Boston’s Belle of Society, how dare she be so inconvenienced. Of course she blamed it all on her father, thinking to herself this was just another example of his persecution against her.

Suffering from near exhaustion and perspiration, which was so unlady like she took a moment to catch her breath and pull herself together in preparation of seeing her father. She knocked once on the door with a faint tap and waited. There was no response. She knocked a second time with more vigor and still no response. In desperation, after everything she had been through just to get there, she took the handle of her umbrella and struck it loudly against the metal door thinking, *Well, that should get their attention.* The door opened and there stood Thomas. “I’m looking for my father, Professor ReMax,” she said.

“Yes, ma’am, he’s in here. Please come in, he would love to see you.” As she entered the first thing she saw was Midnight, but seeing him this time gave her comfort instead of fear.

She looked at her brother sitting next to the frail white haired man as both men stood to greet her. “Tasha, honey, it’s been so long and I am so sorry for all the years I have missed being with you. Can you ever forgive me?” begged the professor. Tears started to roll down her face as she stood quietly before her father. He dried the wetness from her cheeks. His face was old and wrinkled and not at all the way she remembered. He was just a shell of an old man and no longer any threat. All the anger she carried towards him all those years simply vanished, she was no longer under his control. He stretched out his arms inviting her in and she hugged her father like she had never hugged him before. For the first time in a very long time she was her humble self and not just a mask for society. She was overtaken with emotions, so much that she didn’t even question the cat. Midnight was very pleased.

Chiptaw had never seen a family reunion like the one the professor and his children were having. They spent the next few days catching up on each other’s lives. One morning, Thomas was having breakfast with them at the hotel when a slender man in his middle forties entered, and sat down in the booth next to them. His name was Anthony Spencer and he was a professional con-man. He heard about the professor’s misfortune when he came into town. It was the talk of the locals. He also heard the man was somewhat of an eccentric and very rich. He sat quietly and listened and realized he had fallen into the sting of a lifetime.

After finishing breakfast the professor decided to show

his son and daughter what was left of the lab and Spencer followed. Although it was only a pile of rubble, they knew how much it meant to their father. They tried to encourage him to continue his research, but he felt his golden years were upon him and he was tired, very, very tired.

When they returned from Duncan's Mountain they made plans to have dinner at Papa and Mama's. Arriving promptly at seven o'clock Jonathan and Tasha met Papa and Mama DellaVecchia. Even Ms. Belle of Society was impressed by the charm of this quaint family Italian restaurant.

"Hey-a professor, you and your family come in and sit-a down. I give-a you the best seat in the house," said Papa cheerfully. Thomas was running a little late, he picked up Telesa and arrived shortly after with Midnight.

"Oh Papa, there's-a Midnight," said Mama. "Come on little boy. You and me we go in the kitchen and get-a you a treat." The happy little feline followed with great expectations. "You such a good boy Midnight. Mama, she-a loves you very much. You one special little boy. Here-a you go, enjoy."

Saturday nights were the busiest and the restaurant was getting crowded. A stranger entered dressed in a silk suit which matched his neatly trimmed hair and mustache. Mama thought *what a fine looking gentleman* and asked, "How many people in-a your party?" He smiled with a smile that melted Mama in her footsteps. "Just one, I'm alone." He was so handsome and had such charisma; she had a hard time keeping her eyes to herself, as she showed him to his table.

"Here-a you go, sir. This be-a good seat for you,"

which just happened to be next to the professor's table. The gentleman looked at her with his dark brown eyes and said, "Mama, please call me Anthony. My name is Anthony Spencer and I'm in town to do some business. Could you possibly tell me where I might find a Professor ReMax?"

Clearly hearing their conversation the professor turned around and inspected the gentleman and announced, "I'm Professor ReMax, sir. How may I assist you?"

The stranger stood, shook his hand and said, "Sir, I've been sent here by some investors to speak with you about your work, but please don't let me interrupt your dinner. If you will be available tomorrow I would appreciate the opportunity to meet with you to discuss their proposal." The professor was suspicious but fascinated so he agreed to meet the following day.

The evening came to an end and as the professor and his guests were leaving, Papa and Mama's only son made a surprise visit. He had flown in from Italy to see his parents. "Hey-a Papa, I'm-a here all the way from the old country," shouted Bruno.

"Hey-a Bruno come to you Papa." They embraced and kissed on each cheek as Papa called Mama who was-a one happy woman.

"Oh my baby boy. Bruno, how-a you been? Why you not call Mama and Papa and tell us you-a coming?" Introductions were made and everyone departed going their separate ways, having enjoyed an evening with family and dear friends.

Laying in bed the professor tossed and turned. He was apprehensive about the next day's meeting. He tried to understand how this man found him after all the trouble he went through to disappear. He was skeptical and untrusting. But a part of him gleamed in the idea of someone carrying on his work. But it couldn't be just anyone.

When morning came he greeted Thomas downstairs and asked him to accompany him to the meeting. Spencer reserved a suite and ordered a light breakfast upon their arrival. Casual conversation ensued. The con-man asked questions about the professor and his family and gathered as much information as possible so he could perfect the sting. But first a seed had to be planted. With precise timing and professionalism Spencer made his presentation.

"Professor, let's get down to business. Sir, I've been sent here by a group of investors who wish to remain anonymous for now, who hold your knowledge and expertise in the highest degree. They are aware of your great accomplishments in the field of genetics. Their desire is to help better the world as we know it and change the future in an effort to benefit mankind. With your knowledge and past successes, this task cannot fail. Of course, they would want you to come on board as a consultant and oversee the research. You will have the best qualified staff that money can buy and a lab with state of the art equipment."

Looking scantly over his glasses at this man he barely knew he asked with uncertainty, "Young man, why do I need investors? I've always financed my own research and I've done so quite well."

Shady Spencer wittingly replied, "Yes sir, and I mean no disrespect, but the fact is your work is too important to continue alone. I'm sure you will agree sir, that you have reached a point in your life when you must make time for yourself and your family. You have an opportunity here to see your research continue without it being a financial burden, while you spend quality time with the ones you love. Time is a priceless gift."

The professor looked at Thomas and nodded his head in agreement and invited a response. "Well, my boy, what do you think about this proposal?" Thomas was not as convinced.

"Maybe you should give this more thought sir, before making a decision." And that's all that was said. Meanwhile, Spencer continued to delve into the professor's past so he would be prepared for their next meeting.

CHAPTER 7

Jonathan and Tasha spent the rest of the day with their father discussing the past twenty years. The aging scientist was reluctant to engage in conversation with his children about this proposal, even though they encouraged him to continue his work. So, later that evening he called Thomas to discuss the possibility of turning over his research. They discussed the pros and cons and the professor decided he needed to know more about these so called investors because his research in the wrong hands could be detrimental to humanity.

Over the next few days Spencer searched on the internet looking up every article and published work of the professor, as well as making inquiries with previous associates. The more he explored, the more he learned. He grew anxious imagining how this sting could be his greatest triumph, and make him very rich. It was time to arrange for a second meeting.

Shady Acres was a typical run of the mill hotel and not especially elegant, so Spencer made reservations at the professor's favorite restaurant. Thomas escorted his colleague and Midnight was not far behind. The majestic cat raced to the kitchen where Mama had a warm bowl of milk waiting for him, served at just the right temperature. They were seated and ordered their meal. Fettuccini Alfredo was the professor's choice. Midnight entered, sat under the table licking his paws and cleaning his face.

"Professor," said Spencer. "I want to thank you for giving me the opportunity for this second meeting." With some hesitation he continued. "Sir, I have consulted with the sponsors and I'm afraid they have decided to venture into other areas of investing. Their decision has nothing to do with you personally, or with your research. To be completely honest sir, I have discovered that these men weren't really interested in your work at all. They were looking only to sell it to the highest bidder. With all sincerity I must apologize. Had I known their true intentions I would have never agreed to be their spokesman. But, I assure you I can always find other investors." Spencer knew exactly what he was doing when he introduced one of the professor's previous associates.

"Sir, I have made contact with Professor Marian Rutherford at the University of Washington. You may recall she was one of your best students. She says you have been such a major influence in her life that she chose to continue in your field. She has a P.H.D. in phylogenetics, ecological genetics, and molecular evolution. She has done research similar to yours and in fact she has even explored human cloning." Of course Spencer never spoke to the woman.

Well, this certainly peaked the interest of the professor. He remembered this student. She graduated with honors at the top of his class. He thought of her often and knew she had potential, and by the sound of it she became everything he expected. Spencer produced an article written by Professor Rutherford on the prospects of human cloning and urged him to read it as he had arranged for a telephone conference with her the following day.

Ready to retire for the evening, they returned to the hotel and the professor inquired of Thomas, his thoughts. "Well sir, I really don't know. It couldn't hurt to at least speak with Professor Rutherford and then you can decide." Looking over at Midnight the elderly man asked, "And what about you my mystical little friend?" only to hear a responsive, "*meow.*"

Awake most of the night, the professor finally fell asleep and dreamed of his children and grandchildren. When he woke an hour later he found Midnight lying across his bed. "Well, hello boy, how are you doing? You know, I just can't decide what I should do. When will it ever be enough? When will I feel the satisfaction that I have done all I can do to help mankind and just let go?" The frisky feline started chanting, "*Meow, meow,*" as he sent the professor a message. "*You have little time left and you must spend it with your family."* He sat back in his chair and caressed the top of the cat's head. "You're absolutely right boy. I will make my decision tomorrow after I speak with Professor Rutherford. Let's go to bed and get some sleep, I'm very tired."

Meanwhile, Spencer spent his evening on his cell phone prepping his associate, Mallory Malone to impersonate Professor Rutherford. She too was an experienced con artist who worked on the wrong side of the tracks—they had been partners before, successful partners. If they pulled this off they would be abundantly rich and she was more than eager to get her share of the mark.

After hours of preparation they were ready and with only a few hours sleep Spencer set up the call at the hotel in room five-o-one. Plugging a speaker into his cell phone he dialed the number. "May I please speak with Professor Rutherford? She is expecting my call. This is Anthony Spencer." They waited patiently as they heard the professor being paged over the intercom.

"Hello," answered a feminine voice which sounded far too young to have been the professor's prodigy student. Not recognizing the voice Spencer grew nervous and asked, "Is this Professor Rutherford?" There was silence. Another female voice followed. "Hello, this is Professor Rutherford. May I help you?" Spencer recognized this voice and was relieved.

"This is Anthony Spencer and I have Professor ReMax here on speaker phone."

The quaint voice of the woman on the other end said, "Yes, professor, I continued to follow your work up until a few years ago when you disappeared. I'm not sure you remember me, but I was once one of your students back at the University."

Taking comfort in speaking with this genius of a young mind he exclaimed, "Yes, I certainly do remember you. I have read some your published articles and I was impressed with your opinion regarding the workings of the fragile-x syndrome. I found it quite interesting." They spent the next thirty minutes discussing the pros and cons of human cloning and she wanted to continue conversing but her schedule would not allow for more time. She apologized and assured the professor that if he elected her to continue with his work, she would be just as dedicated and devoted as he, and she was very excited about the opportunity to follow in his footsteps.

They said their goodbye's and thanked each other for the meeting and the conversation ended. Spencer disconnected the phone as the professor sat back in his chair, still questioning if he should hand over his life's work. But, he felt very confident with Professor Rutherford, and he knew from his past experiences with her, that if anyone could carry on his research to the magnitude of his expectations, it would certainly be Marian Rutherford.

However, still uncertain he looked to Thomas for endorsement who nodded his head in agreement at which time the professor agreed to the proposal. "Thank you, sir," said Spencer. "I'm sure Professor Rutherford will be all you expect her to be, but we have one remaining problem."

With a dreadful look the professor rose out of his chair and asked, "And what might that be Mr. Spencer?"

This was the critical moment, Spencer had to be convincing. "Well, sir, since we have lost the investors for financial support.... well, there just isn't enough funding available to set up the lab and relocate Professor Rutherford. It will take time to find other investors."

With a pleasant smile he looked over his glasses and replied, "My boy, money is no object. Tell me what you need and I will make it happen." Spencer succeeded and the sting was almost complete. "Well, sir, with the help of Professor Rutherford, I have already calculated the estimated cost for the next five years but that doesn't include setting up the lab. I'm searching for co-sponsors to invest, but it's going to take a lot of capital to get the lab up and running."

The professor returned to his seat and said, "Young man, I have no intentions of employing any financiers. My work is confidential. I will provide whatever funds will be necessary. I will make arrangements to distribute ten million dollars to get this project off the ground. Once I see that Professor Rutherford is all that I anticipate, I will make arrangements to totally support the lab."

Spencer never dreamed he could con anyone out of this much money. The professor continued, "I'll have my lawyers draw up the necessary papers, for everyone's protection of course, and we'll have another meeting with Professor Rutherford." Thinking quickly Spencer intercepted, "Sir, I would really like to get started as soon as possible. There's a lot to be done. I'm thinking we should rebuild here, right on Duncan's Mountain. Can you advance a portion of the funds prior to signing the contracts?" Spencer had totally gained the trust of this not so trusting man and he agreed to a cash advance of one million dollars. "Yes, my boy. I should be able to have the money for you in about two weeks. You're absolutely correct. It will take the lawyer's months to draw up the contracts."

The deal was made and sealed with a handshake. In two weeks Spencer would have a million dollars with more to follow if he played his cards right.

Spencer called Mallory. "Hey, what was the meaning of the other voice on the phone?" he asked.

"That wasn't part of the plan. But, regardless we're in and he has taken the bait." She explained, "My sister's kid picked up the phone but fortunately she didn't say anything but hello."

"Well, don't let it happen again. We may have to set up another meeting. Be sure you're ready."

That evening the professor and his family were dining at Papa and Mama's, enjoying the comforts of pasta and the company of one another. Jonathan looked at his father and asked, "Dad, you know we have spent a lot of time trying to catch up over the past week and it's been wonderful. Why don't you come back with me to New York and meet your grandson and great grandchildren?"

Tasha was swift to intercept, "Yes, that's a marvelous idea. I have to get back and prepare for Amanda Renee's debut. Say, Jonathan why don't we have a big family reunion with all of us at Martha's Vineyard? You can arrange for the kids to meet you there and Dad can meet everyone at the same time."

Jonathan nodded his head in agreement and asked his father, "Well, what do you say Dad?" Tears of joy trickled down the cheeks of the professor. His aging face grew brighter as he graciously accepted their invitation.

"Fine," said Tasha, "then we'll see you, one week from today. I'll make all the arrangements and introduce you to only the finest people."

Jonathan shook his head, laughed and said, "Tasha, this is a family get together, remember?"

"Yes, I know. I just thought I would introduce Dad to some important people."

The professor confessed, "Honey that really isn't necessary. I would just like to spend time with my family, if that's okay." She surrendered the idea but promised him it would be a social gathering he would never forget.

He said, "I'm sure it will, my dear. I'm sure it will."

Over the next few days Thomas spent little time with the professor who was preparing to visit Boston. But, on the day before he was supposed to leave, they met for lunch at the local diner. "Thomas," whispered the professor his voice shaking with emotion. "I want to thank you for all your help and dedication. Until you and, of course Midnight, came into my life, I really didn't have a life. I can't explain how I'm feeling right now, but I know you understand how important my work has been, and you have been completely loyal and supportive. Perhaps Professor Rutherford will keep you on, if you're interested my boy."

Thomas, with plenty of his own emotional turmoil, relayed to the professor, "Sir, I have thoroughly enjoyed working with you and I am so thrilled you have decided to spend time with your family. My plans are to ask Telesa to marry me."

"Well, it's about time my boy, it's about time. But what about after you're married?"

With a look of uncertainty Thomas replied, "Well, since she doesn't ever want to leave Chiptaw, I guess I'll find something to do here. Perhaps I will consider working for the professor." Finishing their lunch they departed with each giving the other a hug that only a father and son should share. Thomas knew he was going to miss this old man who had been more like a father than a mentor.

Chapter 8

Thomas checked out of the Shady Acres and moved back into his one room apartment, which was just down the street from Telesa. He and Midnight were close to the woman they loved and he didn't waste any time purchasing the ring, an elegant three carat diamond engagement ring. He made quite a bit of money working for the professor and he was more than anxious to ask the woman he loved to marry him.

The time and place had to be just right, and what would be more perfect than proposing where they first met, at Papa and Mamas.

Arrangements were made for Saturday night and

everyone at the restaurant played a part. A private dining room was reserved. Candles glowed brightly in the darkness of the dimly lit room. The table cloth, made of fine silk all the way from Italy, lay evenly across the glass encased top. Special dinnerware trimmed in gold, for this very special occasion, covered the silky white cloth.

Thomas was dressed in his brand new suit, which complimented his dark hair and mustache. As he entered the room where Telesa was waiting he noticed how her velvet blue dress matched perfectly with her sapphire blue eyes. At that moment he realized he was the luckiest man alive. Midnight made his grand appearance wearing a solid white bow tie wrapped snuggly around his neck.

"My, don't you boys look handsome tonight," she beamed. Violinists followed playing their favorite romantic love songs. A chilled bottle of champagne sat next to the table. Tall, slendor champagne flutes with their edges trimmed in gold, left the table setting flawless.

Papa and Mama watched Thomas take her left hand, get down on one knee and place her hand in his and recite, "Telesa, my love, you are the other half of me and you make me whole. I have adored you from the first moment I saw you come out of Papa and Mama's kitchen. You are my soul mate and I love you with all my heart. Will you marry me and honor me by becoming my wife?"

With joyful tears streaming down her blushing red cheeks she jumped up and shouted, "Yes, yes, yes. I'll marry you, Thomas Sheffield." They embraced and kissed. With one big leap Midnight was wedged between them and they gladly accepted his presence.

"Yes, Midnight, I'll be marrying you too," she laughed as she stroked his soft black fur. The celebration continued with a toast of champagne as their adopted family applauded; they were formally engaged.

Meanwhile, the professor flew into Martha's Vineyard looking forward to the family reunion. Of course Tasha had only the best caterers and it was a most beautiful day. The air was fresh and invigorating. Birds were singing and children were playing. You could hear the waves striking gently against the jagged gray rocks, and the reflection of the ocean tinted the deep blue sky. Jonathan started the introductions by lining up his lineage, presenting each one by name along with a short synopsis.

"Dad, this is my son, Robert, he's thirty one and a successful commercial pilot. This is his wife, Lorraine and they've been married fourteen years. They have three children. This is their youngest, Joshua. He's nine and we have nicknamed him, 'Oops.' When he was five he was thrown out of the back window of a car but he wasn't hurt. He stood up and shook himself off and said, 'Oops,' so we've been calling him 'Oops' ever since. And this is Catherine Louise, their only daughter. She's ten and was named after her grandmother. And last but not least this is Christopher. He's twelve and our designated juvenile delinquent. If there's trouble, he'll find it."

Tasha introduced her family. "Dad, you already know Steven and these are our two daughters, Rose Marie and Amanda Renee. Rose Marie is married to Tim and they are proud parents of twin girls, Rebecca and Teri Ann. Tim couldn't be here today as he had a prior commitment. He sends his apologies. And this is our youngest, Amanda Renee and she is turning sweet sixteen next week and about to embark on her very own debutante ball."

The professor greeted each of them individually by giving them a big hug.

He told them how wonderful it was for him to finally meet them and how happy he was to be their grandfather and great grandfather. This was indeed a most spectacular day, but as the hour grew late the professor had to excuse himself and return to the hotel.

He was weary from all the day's festivities so he laid down to rest. Upon closing his eyes he felt something jump on the sofa next to him. As his tired eyes opened he saw Midnight, who was rubbing his head against the professor's side and purring loudly. "Well, hello Midnight. Nice of you to visit. Say, how is Thomas doing?" The cat responded with a loud *"Meow."*

The professor commenced petting his little companion when he received a message. *"It's time professor."* He understood as he nodded his head and settled in on the sofa and closed his eyes for the very last time, and the angels came and took him home. He was finally at peace.

The news of his passing was not surprising to his children. They cherished the short time they spent with this old man, their father. Their feelings of anger and abandonment were in the past. They treasured only the recent memories of the time they shared with 'Dad.'

Thomas was with Telesa when he received the call about the professor's passing. Jonathan thanked him for everything and especially for getting him in contact with his family. As the saddened lab assistant laid down the receiver his eyes started to tear and Telesa knew the news was about the professor. She took him in her arms to comfort him and they both cried at the loss of this incredible man. Midnight sitting nearby shared in their grief shedding his own tears in a most feline fashion.

Meanwhile, Anthony Spencer was waiting patiently for his money as the week had come and gone, unbeknownst that his mark had departed this life. He stayed in town a few more days waiting for a word from the professor. When he didn't receive word he contacted Thomas.

Knock, knock, knock, sounded the door. Telesa answered. She couldn't keep from staring at his tall handsome build. "May I help you?" she asked.

"Yes, I'm looking for Thomas Sheffied. Would he happen to be here? I have some business with the professor and I was getting concerned since I haven't heard from him."

He gazed endlessly into her sapphire blue eyes. "Oh, I guess you haven't heard. He passed away while visiting his family in Boston." The look on Spencer's face was devastating. Not for the loss of the professor but for the loss of his mark. Thomas entered the room.

"Mr. Spencer, I was going to contact you but we just got the news about the professor."

He invited him in and they sat and talked. The con-man was desperate to find out the whereabouts of his money.

"Thomas, you know I have worked very hard to get the lab up and running and I need the cash promised by the professor. Do you know how I can obtain that money?" Puzzled, Thomas responds, "No, I'm afraid I don't, but perhaps his son may know something. Although, this really isn't the time to bring up the subject since they're getting ready to bury their father."

Midnight, sitting on the floor next to Telesa, begins to growl and stare persistently at Spencer. She tries to soothe the enraged feline when Thomas receives a message. *"This is a dangerous man and he cannot be trusted. He must leave and he must leave now."* Without hesitation or explanation Thomas stood and announced, "Spencer, let me show you to the door. You'll be leaving now."

Shocked, Telesa says, "Thomas, how rude," apologizing as they escorted out their unwelcome guest. "That's fine Miss, perhaps this isn't the appropriate time. Please extend my condolences to the professor's family."

As he left she turned and saw Thomas sitting on the couch with Midnight in his lap, each staring at the other looking like they were carrying on a conversation. "Thomas Sheffield, was that necessary? Why were you so rude to that nice gentleman?"

He looked at her and said, "Trust me, I have my reasons. That so called gentleman is nothing more than a con-man and he's been setting up the professor for just that, a con, to steel his money under false pretenses. He's good, very good, but we have figured him out and just in time."

"We?" she asked.

He was caught off guard. "Don't worry honey, I'll handle it, no matter what it takes," and nothing further was said.

The next day Jonathan was back in his office in Manhattan going through his father's briefcase when he came across a large sum of cash, a million dollars to be exact. He knew his father was an eccentric but why would he keep so much money lying around? He called Thomas hoping to find some answers.

"Hello, Thomas, this is Jonathan. I was going through some of Dad's things and I came across a huge sum of cash. Would you know anything about it?"

"Jonathan, I'm glad you called. I was going to call and warn you about this Spencer guy. I just found out that the so called business dealings he had with the professor to rebuild the lab was just a con, a way to extort money. This guy came into town just after the explosion and after hearing about it he tried to take advantage of the professor's tragedy. He played it to the hilt and even conjured up one of his old students to be part of the con using an accomplice to impersonate her. This guy really did his home work. He showed up here yesterday, wanting to know if I knew where the money was that the professor was going to advance him. After I told him of his passing he was so persistent about getting the cash, it made me suspicious. That's when I realized he was just a con-man."

Jonathan wasn't surprised. He dealt with people like this all the time and he spent most of his life defending them, but this was different. This was personal and involved his family and even though the sting wasn't complete, Jonathan wanted revenge. To such an extent he was on the next plane to Virginia.

Arriving in Roanoke, he rented a car, drove to Chiptaw, and checked into the Shady Acres. He wanted to get as much information as possible about this Anthony Spencer, if in fact, that was his real name. But he also had another purpose for the trip. After getting settled, he phoned Thomas and asked if he and Telesa would meet him at Papa and Mama's for dinner. They met at around seven o'clock and as usual Midnight followed.

They were greeted by Bruno DellaVecchia who was still visiting from Italy. "Thomas and Telesa, how-a are you? And there is-a Midnight. Go on boy, Mama she's-a in the kitchen and she's-a waiting for you." Midnight pounced into Mama's arms.

"Hey-a Midnight, you-a Mama's boy. How-a you been?"

Papa saw the happy couple waiting up front and motioned for them to come his way as they had a special guest waiting. Another guest arrived. It was Spencer. He heard Jonathan was in town and hence a new mark.

Midnight kept a watchful eye. Jonathan invited Papa and Mama to join them as he poured each a glass of wine and stood to make a toast. "I want to thank all of you for the wonderful things you've done for my father. He spoke very highly of you during the short time we spent together. Thomas, his life changed when you became a part of it, and for that I will be forever grateful. I don't know exactly how but you were the key to bringing our family together again." He raised his glass and said, "A toast to Telesa and Thomas. May they share many happy years together."

The clinking of wine glasses filled the room. "Thomas, in celebration of your marriage to Telesa and your dedication to my father and his work, I wish to give you this gift." Taking a sealed envelope from his pocket he handed it to Thomas. "Jonathan, I appreciate the gesture but you really didn't have to ... " He stopped talking and gazed at the check that had so many zero's he lost count. "Jonathan, I really can't accept this ... I mean no disrespect but I just can't ... " Mama interrupted.

"Thomas, what's-a matter with you? This man he's-a giving you a wedding gift, just say thank you."

Thomas looked at Telesa and handed her the check and when she saw the amount she blurted out, "A million dollars?" Papa said, "Did-a she say a million dollars?"

Mama answered, "Yes she said-a million dollars." Everyone gathered around the happy couple and carefully examined the check.

Papa was so excited he ran through the restaurant and announced, "He just got a million dollars for his-a wedding gift. Isn't that-a nice?"

Spencer sitting nearby got up from the table and asked Bruno, "Who's getting married?" Bruno said, "It's-a Thomas and Telesa."

Midnight started to growl and hiss at Spencer. There was so much commotion everyone left the dining room to see what was going on only to find Spencer pinned up against the wall with Midnight's teeth and claws extended.

Fearing the cat was going to attack, he hollered, "Will somebody get that crazy animal away from me?"

Thomas started to move towards him when Midnight

sent him a message. *"Be careful, he has a gun."* Midnight backed off as Spencer tried to compose himself.

When Jonathan came closer he realized this was the man he came to town to see. He lunged towards him and grabbed the lapel of his jacket. "You good for nothing bum. How dare you try and con my father. Just who do you think you are?" Suddenly Jonathan felt the nozzle of a gun in his side.

"I'm the man with the gun and if you don't let go of me right now I'm going to send you to meet your maker." Jonathan released his grip and stepped backwards.

Thomas looked at Telesa. She was petrified. Midnight kept growling and hissing as Spencer pointed the gun directly at him, when all at once an unseen force took hold of the gun and flung it across the room. Bruno was quick to retrieve it and hold it on Spencer.

It took a while for things to calm down and Mama said, "We need to call the police and have-a that man arrested. He is-a no good and he can-a never come here again."

Jonathan said, "No, Mama. I don't want the police involved. I'll take care of this myself." He motioned to Bruno to let him go. Trying to make light of the situation Papa said, "Hey, after all, it's not-a every day somebody gets a million dollar wedding gift and a gun fight all in the same day." They laughed and they cried; this had indeed been a memorable day for Chiptaw.

Chapter 9

Spencer went into hiding but knew he'd invested way too much time and his own money to not make a score. One way or another he was going to get something out of somebody. If he could find the professor's research, he could sell it on the black market and still become very rich. So, his search began.

He broke into the professor's suite and questioned if the eccentric old man would have left something so valuable lying around his room. He had to think. Where would he have hidden something so important? Where would it be the safest and the least obvious? He came upon an oddly shaped key with a note attached. It said, 'Duncan's

Mountain, forty paces north, twenty paces east, ten paces south, Telesa and picnic.' *But what did it mean?*

The key had to open something. He found a briefcase buried in the closet and tried the key but it didn't fit. Tearing the room apart he kept looking, thinking the professor may have hidden it in the wall. He was making far too much noise and had to be careful. After what seemed like hours he left with only the key and a clue.

Shortlyafter, Jonathan and Thomas entered the room. Seeing the mess they knew Spencer had been there looking for anything to make a dollar. They weren't surprised. This man had to be stopped. Jonathan asked, "What do you think he was after?" With a worried look Thomas walked over to the dresser and pulled out the drawer. "What?" asked Jonathan. Feeling underneath and not finding what he was looking for he said, "Jonathan, he's got the key to the professor's safe. If he gets his hands on that safe, well, I hate to think what he'll do with the professor's research."

"We'll just have to stop him. Where is the safe?"

Thomas hesitated, "I don't know. The professor never said and I didn't ask. He only told me about the key."

They left the hotel to find Spencer. They had to enlist some help so they stopped to speak to Bruno. Jonathan knew this man very well, even though they had met only once. He knew his type and what he was capable of doing if the price were right. After a short meeting the deal was made.

Chiptaw was a small town and there weren't many places where a man like Spencer could hide. After a careful search, they couldn't find him. They even thought he may have left town. But they knew if there was any way for this man to make a buck he wasn't going anywhere.

Thomas and Midnight returned home to have a chat. If anyone could find a needle in a haystack, this magical feline could. "Little buddy, we have to find Spencer. He has the key to the professor's safe and I don't know where the safe is and if Spencer gets his hands on it, well, you know."

Midnight stretched and yawned and relayed a message, *"I know the location of the safe. I was with the professor when he buried it near the lab."* With a sigh of relief Thomas said, "Good, let's get up there and find it before Spencer does."

They jumped in the Mustang and took a ride up Duncan's Mountain. It was just about dawn when they arrived. You could still smell the burnt wood piled high over layers of melted steel. Thomas got out of the car, looked around and said, "Well, I don't see Spencer anywhere. Maybe we've beaten him here, you think?"

Midnight followed along as they walked cautiously over the fallen debris, all of a sudden the cat stopped and blurted out a loud, *"Meow."* Thomas turned and looked behind him seeing a large empty hole as he received another message. *"It was here Thomas but it's gone now."* Disappointed Thomas asked, "What are we going to do now Midnight?"

Returning to town they met up with Jonathan and Bruno. All hope of finding Spencer was lost until the phone rang and the man on the other end identified himself as the missing con-man and he wanted to speak to Thomas. Taking the receiver and placing it to his ear he said, "This is Thomas, what do you want?"

There was silence and then Spencer started to speak. "I have the professor's research. Amazing how I found it, you know. Do you want me to tell you how I found out where it was buried? It's a beautiful story."

Thomas replied, "Go ahead."

With a wave of wickedness Spencer chuckled and said, "I have your sweet Telesa with me and she is very, very sweet if you know what I mean."

Thomas could not contain his fury. "I'll get you Spencer. If you harm one hair on her head I'll kill you."

Spencer said, "Calm down. She's safe and I haven't touched her ... yet. You know that professor friend of yours was pretty clever. He left a clue with a key and it was your sweet little girlfriend who helped me find the safe."

But how is that possible? he wondered. *She knew nothing about the professor's work.* Spencer laughed, "The clue was very obvious once she explained it to me. Do you remember the picnic on Duncan's Mountain with the professor?"

"Yes, but what does that have to do with anything?"

Spencer cackled, "You're not as smart as I thought Thomas. The professor left instructions on how to find the safe from the location of your picnic. Once your lovely lady showed me the spot I found the safe."

"How do I know you have Telesa, and how do I know, you really have the professor's research?"

Spencer grabbed the frightened young woman by the arm and handed her the phone and said, "Tell him."

She took the phone and started to cry. "Thomas, I'm okay and I'm sorry, but he did find the safe and he does have the professor's research. I didn't know."

Thomas tried to console her when Spencer seized the phone. "Now, listen up. The million dollars you received as a wedding gift belongs to me. And if I don't see that money by tomorrow night, your sweetheart will never come home. I get the money, you get the girl. I'd say that's a pretty fair bargain, wouldn't you?"

"And what about the professors research, is that part of the deal too?"

"Oh, no, I intend to sell that to the highest bidder. Listen you, I want my money and I want it now or this sweet young thing will never be yours." The conversation ended with a dial tone.

The three men gathered around and Thomas asked, "Jonathan, I don't want to give into this guy, but what about Telesa?" The New York lawyer looked at Bruno and nodded his head and without saying a word Bruno left knowing it was time to do what he did best. "Don't worry Thomas, we'll find her," reassured Jonathan.

Returning home Thomas and his feline friend sat down to think. The room was empty and lonely without Telesa. "Midnight, isn't there something you can do to help me find her?" A telepathic message followed, *"I can't find her if we keep sitting around here feeling sorry for ourselves. Get up and let's go."*

Midnight loved to ride in the Mustang, even though he had his own mode of transportation. In fact, Thomas often wondered how long it would be before his little buddy would be driving. *"Soon,"* chuckled the feisty feline.

They rode around for hours. "Where, can they be?" bellowed Thomas. Leaving the city below they traveled up Duncan's Mountain. Midnight started getting excited. "What is it, boy?" A message followed. *"They're nearby, keep driving."* They came upon a dilapidated shack. *"Stop, they're here."* Bringing the car to a halt at the end of a dirt road, he turns off the engine and headlights. He and the cat approach the weather beaten shack and see a dimmed lantern burning through the broken window. They listen and hear a female voice.

"Spencer, you will never get away with this insane act. They will find you, and to think I thought you were so incredibly handsome and flawless. Boy was I wrong." It was Telesa and she was safe, at least for now. Thomas returned to the car and called the professor's son while his loyal feline went on the prowl.

Forty-five minutes later Jonathan and Bruno arrived. Thomas was waiting in his car at the end of the road about a quarter mile from the old house. "Jonathan, she's in the shack with Spencer. I don't know if he has the professor's research, I couldn't tell." They proceeded up the winding road. It was pitch black and hard to see. They had to be careful. If Spencer got wind they were outside, he may harm Telesa and flee. Bruno went around back as Thomas and Jonathan looked through the front window. Midnight sitting in the corner watched as Spencer paced back and forth in front of him. His collar glows and Thomas receives a message.

"She's tied to a chair on the other side of the room. She's gagged but she's okay. She knows I'm here and she can see me. Spencer cannot. You must be careful Thomas, he is a very dangerous man."

They waited for the opportune moment to enter.

Midnight disappeared and reappeared hissing and growling, clawing at Spencer's back. Thomas and Jonathan entered through the front and Bruno through the rear. Bruno placed Spencer in a headlock as Midnight jumped off. They tumbled to the floor and struggled. Spencer pulled his gun and a shot was fired and then a second and third. Stray shots ricocheted around the room. Bruno finally got the gun away from Spencer and held it flat against his head just begging him to make a move so he would have a reason to shoot.

Thomas ran to Telesa. "Oh, no, she's been hit," he cried. "Call 911, call 911!" he shouted. One of the stray bullets pierced her lower abdomen and she was bleeding out. Thomas quickly untied her, removed the gag from around her mouth and laid her flat on the floor. She was unconscious. He ripped off his shirt, tore it into strips to pack the wound.

Midnight stood by her side, placed his paws on the pieces of cloth filling with blood. As his collar lit up, the area of the wound began to glow and radiate heat. She started to come to and Midnight released his paws and with pure exhaustion, lay down beside her.

"Thomas," she said with a faint voice. "What happened? I feel so strange." He removed the pieces of cloth; there were no signs of injury. She had been healed. Her guardian angel saved her. He helped her to her feet and held her tightly. No one understood what just happened, other than they witnessed a miracle, a true miracle. Thomas picked up his little buddy and they went home.

Jonathan and Bruno stayed behind with Spencer. "You

know what to do," said Jonathan. "I don't want to know when, where or how, only that it's been done." Spencer pleaded for his life. "You should-a thought about that before-a you mess with Telesa," growled the Italian hit man. "You-a coming with me."

They drove down the mountain and dropped off Jonathan. Spencer was tied and gagged and there was no way he was going to escape. Knowing his fate he continued to beg for mercy with moans of desperation but there was no stopping Bruno. He was going to do what he did best.

Chapter 10

Thomas watched over Telesa all night as she slept. She awoke just before dawn. After last night they didn't want to risk losing each other ever again so they decided not to wait to get married. They looked for Midnight, he was gone, but Thomas knew his little buddy was alright.

The lake located at the base of Duncan's Mountain was one of the deepest lakes in Virginia and a major portion was surrounded by thick brush. Spencer, still tied and gagged, was being pushed by Bruno through the dense foliage, often falling down. "Get up you bum," said Bruno. "Keep-a moving." They continued walking through the bushy terrain until they reached the waters edge. Bruno removed the gag from Spencer's mouth and there was silence. There was a chill in the air but not enough to cool the sweat on Spencer's brow.

Dawn was slowly approaching. The moon lit night cast down its reflection over the water. The stars in the sky dazzled in the darkness. They stood in silence with Bruno holding a gun on Spencer. Moments passed when Midnight appeared. He sat dauntlessly on a huge bolder with the glimmer of the moon showing a silhouette of his feline physique. As his collar illuminated Bruno watched and was amazed.

Spencer tried to run, while Bruno looked away, only to be knocked down by the six foot mafia hit man. "Where do you think-a you going?" Bruno received a telepathic message from Midnight. "*Do not harm this man. He will get his just reward. Untie his hands and leave him here. Go back and tell Jonathan the job is done.*" He nodded his head in agreement and untied Spencer.

"What, you're letting me go?" asked the con-man. There was no reply. Bruno pointed his finger towards the forest and Spencer ran. He ran like he had never run before.

The brush was thick and binding. It was difficult to tell which direction he should go. He became confused and disoriented. He was lost. Midnight followed close behind. Spencer staggered through the woods for hours, than realized he was going around in circles. He started to panic. He was not a woodsman. He knew nothing about the great outdoors or how to survive. He stops to rest and regain his focus. In the distance he hears the roar of a mountain lion and it's coming closer. He had no weapons to defend himself and he was scared, more than when Bruno had the gun to his head. He knew he couldn't just sit there and wait. He had to keep moving.

Rising to his feet he steps back into a pile of branches. He hears 'snap' and feels excruciating pain. His right ankle is snared in a large bear trap. The pain was intense as he tried to free his foot. It was no use. The mountain lion was drawing near. He could smell his blood. The roar grew louder and louder and then there was complete silence. Spencer looked all around trying to be prepared for the attack. The anticipation was too much. He feared for his life.

As minutes pass he loses more blood. With his foot entangled in the metal vice he scoots over to a nearby bolder. His strength was almost gone. He laid back and closed his eyes. He knew he was going to die. He prayed like he had never prayed before. He cried, "God, please forgive me for all the wrong I've done in my life and for all the people I've hurt. I am truly sorry." The burden on his heart was lifted as the angel of death escorted him to who knows where. After Spencer succumbed, Midnight came to him, placed his paw on his shoulder wishing him a peaceful journey.

Bruno returned to town and went to see Jonathan. When he knocked on the door it opened and there sat Midnight. The big city lawyer was on the phone trying to settle his father's estate. The hired hit man entered and gave a positive nod letting him know the job was done. Jonathan hung up the phone and started to write a check. The big Italian man looked at the mystical black cat staring at him and said, "I can't take-a you money because

I didn't take out Spencer but I know he's-a dead. I just didn't do it." He was shocked. He knew men like Bruno and even if he didn't do the job he would have said he did just to get the money.

The collar around Midnight's neck started to glow as Jonathan received a message, "*Spencer is dead and Bruno is being honest because its the right thing to do.*" He understood and nothing else was said.

Plans were made that evening to gather at Papa and Mama's as Jonathan had a surprise for everyone before he returned to Manhattan. Telesa looked beautiful in her black dress, with a string of white pearls draped loosely around her neck. She had only vague memories of her recent ordeal. Some things were best just left alone so it was never discussed.

After everyone was seated, Jonathan stood and raised his glass of wine to make a toast to the people of Chiptaw. "Here's to Papa and Mama for the wonderful friendship you formed with my father and with me, not to mention this delicious food." The guest at the table laughed and applauded.

"And here's to Thomas and Telesa, may they have a long and happy life together. And here's to Bruno DellaVecchia for being a good friend, cheers." The clinking of wine glasses resonated around the room as Jonathan continued, "Papa and Mama, I have been settling my father's estate and I am pleased to tell you, he has remembered you in his will. He has left each of you five hundred thousand dollars."

Mama, she started to cry, Papa took her in his arms and they cried together. They never dreamed they would receive such a generous gift. They were very, very grateful. Jonathan took a large packet out of his dress jacket and handed it to Bruno, telling him, "This is your reward for helping rescue Telesa." Bruno wasn't expecting anything but gladly accepted the envelope which contained fifty thousand dollars. Jonathan looked at the young couple sitting at the table and with great admiration announced, "My father also remembered you, leaving you a gift of one million dollars." This was indeed a happy day in Chiptaw.

A few weeks pass and final arrangements were being made for the wedding. Even though they had enough money to last them two lifetimes they were not spendthrifts. They wanted a simple wedding with just family and friends. The local Methodist Church where Telesa and her family were members provided the finest setting. They would have a traditional wedding and be married by the local pastor, but they would also recite their own vows.

She was a beautiful bride as she walked elegantly down the aisle holding her fathers arm. She was a vision of loveliness in her white satin dress covered with layers of lace flowing gracefully along the floor. Thomas stood at the alter dressed in a black tux and tie gazing with desire at his bride. Midnight, acting as the ring bearer, wearing a white bow tie around his neck, carried the bride and grooms rings. The pastor began the ceremony as they stood before God and all the witnesses and exchanged their vows. With a passionate kiss they were pronounced husband and wife and introduced as Mr. and Mrs. Sheffield.

Jonathan returned to Manhattan and, working late one night, he was visited once again by the magical feline. Sitting at his desk, he heard that all too familiar "*Meow*" and while walking towards the door, it opened. There sat the proverbial little feline who had found a special place in the heart of this troubled man.

"Midnight, I knew it was you." Inviting him in, the cat took one upward plunge and landed on top of his paper covered desk, knocking everything on the floor. "Some things never change," he chuckled as he sat in his chair and stared out the window at the city lights below.

The cat's collar started to glow as he sent a message to Jonathan. "*By now you know I have special powers, which were given to me through your father's research.*" Fearful of what he was hearing, he turned around his chair and stared as the cat's message continued. "*His research has to carry on because I need help to return home. But, until then, I am destined to protect the innocents. Even though Spencer used Professor Rutherford as a player in his scam, she wasn't a part of it and she is the most logical person to take over your father's work. I will always be there to make sure it stays out of the wrong hands.*"

Jonathan stood and placed his hands in his pockets and paced back and forth in front of the window. "*Jonathan, I am what I am. Do not fear me. I am not a monster. I am a product of your father, and if I can trust you, then you should trust me.*"

He sat down again and placed the cat on his lap, examining the collar; it was solid and clear, made of a material he didn't recognize. As he tried to remove it Midnight suddenly disappeared and reappeared across the room. "*Meow.*" Jonathan couldn't believe what he was seeing.

His body started to shake from the Parkinson's and his thoughts were blurred. He fell to the floor as the cat paced anxiously around him. Just then Midnight placed both paws on the frightened man's shoulders, one on each side, and the shaking stopped. He was calmed by the gentleness of this mystic being. "You really can communicate with me. What did you do to make me feel better?" he asked. With a faint "*meow*" the cat collapsed as all the energy drained from his body. "Are you okay? Tell me what to do so I can help you," he begged. But there was no response.

He placed the cat in his jacket and took him home, where he rested the remainder of the night. When morning came, Jonathan climbed out of bed without any pain. This was most unusual. The pain was always worse in the morning. He stretched and yawned and realized he's never slept better. He wondered, *What was going on?* Looking in the mirror, his face seemed brighter and he felt lighter, like he had been reborn. Searching for Midnight, he couldn't find him, but he didn't worry. He knew the little cat would be just fine.

Weeks pass and Jonathan gives more thought to Midnight's suggestion about his father's research. His regularly scheduled doctor's visit was at one o'clock so he caught a cab and arrived at Doctor Merritt's office. "Jonathan, come in and have a seat. Your blood work has come back and well, it's a mystery."

With a troubled look he asked, "What's wrong?"

"Don't worry its good news. I can't explain it but according to these test, you haven't any signs of Parkinson's." Jonathan was astounded.

"You mean I'm cured?"

With a nod of his head the doctor replied, "That's what I mean and I can't tell you how or why. I've never seen anything like it, and simply put, it's a miracle." This was great news. Jonathan had a second chance at life thanks to a little feline named Midnight.

Chapter 11

Remembering the cat's quest to return home, the least Jonathan could do was think about handing over his father's research to Professor Rutherford. He contacted the University of Washington and made arrangements to meet her the following week.

His flight from New York was miserable as winter introduced herself with a major ice storm, the worst in ten years. Upon arriving in Washington, power outages were the biggest concern. Fire places were burning to generate heat. Those without this luxury were burning logs in barrels, along with anything else they could find. It was cold, very, very cold.

Looting was a problem and the police did all they could to stop the stealing. It was a difficult time. However, the University had power, thanks to their back up generators. He went to the front desk and paged Professor Rutherford. A woman in her early fifties approached him, and seeing her name tag he introduced himself. She was an attractive woman with dark brown shoulder length hair. She was plain and simple, a natural beauty. She carried herself well and Jonathan could see that Midnight was correct. She was the right choice and he sensed it as soon as he saw her. They agreed to meet for dinner that evening.

Trying to find a hotel in the midst of the ice storm was challenging. He flagged down a cab and rode around for sometime before finding a hotel on the Upper East Side who had power. After checking in he took a hot shower, trying desperately to shake off the cold. As he warmed up he sat on the bed and started looking through his father's notes. Of course he didn't understand what he was reading but he knew enough to realize his father had been trying to clone human beings.

He thought, *Dad what did you get yourself into?* Reading on, he came across a notation about a cat. Trying to understand the technical jargon was like reading gibberish, except the part about the cat who fell into a vat of chemicals and became very sick. He was put into a chamber and exposed to a series of lights and boom, he's magical? *This was total nonsense*, he concluded as he placed the files in the briefcase and left for the restaurant.

It was about eight o'clock when the professor arrived. Jonathan requested a private table in the rear of the restaurant. She entered wearing a navy blue dress with matching heels. The dress was simple but she looked radiant, much different than when he saw her earlier in hospital scrubs. Taking her chair, he helped her to her seat and ordered a bottle of wine. She looked at him across the table and smiled. He was quite handsome in his blue suit and red silk tie, but she had to keep her mind on business.

"Professor Rutherford," started Jonathan. "Please call me Marian," she insisted. Jonathan became somewhat tongue tied as he proceeded. "Marian, I appreciate you meeting me with your busy schedule. I know you were one of my father's favorite students when he used to teach at the University and I know you were in the top of his class. I must say, all your accomplishments in genetics really left an impression on him and after having met you I can see why he was so fond of you." Of course he never discussed any such thing with his father.

She sat still, trying to regain her composure. She wasn't accustomed to receiving such compliments and didn't quite know how to react.

"So, how is the professor Jonathan?" she asked.

"He passed away recently. That's one of the reason's I wanted to meet with you."

She extended her condolences. "I'm so sorry to hear of your loss. I have great admiration for your father. He taught me many things. In fact I owe him my career in genetics. If it wasn't for him and his confidence in me I wouldn't be where I am today," she said.

"Thank you." He studied her, speculating if he was making the right decision. Frankly, he'd just met the woman, and he wasn't going to turn over his father's life's work to just anyone. The turmoil he felt inside was met head on when he received another message from Midnight. "*You must give the research to Professor Rutherford if you want to help me.*" He made his decision. "I wanted to discuss the possibility of you taking over my father's research. But, I have to warn you, when you read what's in these papers you may decide you're not interested, in which case, I fully understand." She was honored to be considered and very excited about reading his research.

They finished dinner and he handed her the briefcase. He looked into her eyes and said, "Please take care of this and don't let anything happen to it, Marian." She took it gently from his hands, touching his skin with the tips of her fingers. There was an obvious attraction between them, but more important matters were at hand. They shared a cab and said goodnight.

Once inside her apartment Marian made a cup of hot tea and sat down at the table and started reading. Within minutes she realized the information on these pages was crucial to her future research as she too was exploring human cloning. She was enthused with how far the professor's research progressed to actually create a living, human clone. This was a hot topic of scientific debate. She was well aware that human cloning had been banned in the United States.

Nevertheless, she was very interested, even though she knew the risk. Reviewing his notes about a lab accident involving a cat sounded fascinating, but a clone of a cat possessing supernatural powers? This was beyond reality and scientifically impossible. But then she remembered what the professor told her many years ago. *'Don't let your scientific intellect prevent you from accepting the impossible because the impossible is always possible.'* She read until almost dawn when she fell asleep.

When she woke she found a beautiful black cat sitting on the bed next to her. She thought she was dreaming. Dragging herself to the shower she rinsed off and started drying herself when she saw the cat's reflection in the mirror, sitting on the bed staring at her unclothed body. She covered herself up and walked towards him. She heard a loud "*meow.*" As she reached down to touch him, his fur was soft and felt like velvet—he was very real. She noticed the collar around his neck and it started to glow, but she wasn't afraid, she was curious. She received a message.

"My name is Midnight. I am the cat cloned by the professor and I need your help to return home."

This is very peculiar she thought. *I'm a scientist and this whole magical cat thing is just too bizarre.* Midnight kept sending her messages.

"I am real and I am communicating with you, whether you want to believe it or not. I can help you with the professor's research, but I need your help to find out what went wrong, so I can return home." She finished dressing, took the briefcase and left.

After arriving at the University she telephoned Jonathan. "Good morning Mr. ReMax. I hope you slept well last night with all the power outages," she said.

"Good morning Marian. Please call me Jonathan.

Yes, it was pretty cold even with the furnace going full blast but remember I'm from New York. I can handle just about anything."

She explained, "I was up most of the night reading your fathers work, which I found very intriguing. Do you have any idea what he was doing?"

"Yes, he was cloning humans."

"And you realize that what he was doing has implications?"

"Yes." There was silence. "Marian, are you there?" he asked.

"Yes, I'm here. At least I think I'm here. I'm not really sure after this morning. Something very strange happened."

Jonathan knew exactly. He asked, "Were you visited by Midnight?" She didn't know what to say. If she admitted she saw the cat it would be against every scientific concept she believed in. It was just impossible; absolutely impossible. "Marian, it's all right, I understand. It took me a while to accept him too." She was obviously interested in continuing his father's work, so they agreed to meet again for dinner.

The ice storm passed and the city was slowly getting back to normal. The wind was still viciously cold. People wrapped in their winter coats and scarves tried desperately to stay warm. The ice was melting and the streets were finally clear enough for traffic to flow again. Jonathan reached the restaurant first and asked for a secluded table.

When Marian arrived, she was escorted by the matradee to where he was sitting. The gentleman waiting for the lady stood and helped her to her seat; took her jacket and placed it on the back of her chair. "So, how was your day Marian?" he asked.

"Well, busy as usual. There's always so much to do and so little time," she replied. "You know Marian, I would certainly understand if you didn't want to carry on with Dad's work because of the legalities. Not to mention the probability of a magical cat." She smiled and said, "It's not the legalities that concern me or the so called magical cat. It's finding a place to continue the research which will provide the funding I'll need in order to carry on the professor's work."

Jonathan returned the smile and with a chuckle said, "Oh, I guess I neglected to tell you that my father would be financing all of the research. He put away over one hundred million dollars to fund his research provided it would be relinquished to someone he could trust. And Ms. Rutherford, he can certainly trust you."

This was totally unexpected. "Jonathan, I can't believe this, it's all a dream. Are you certain I'm the one?" she inquired.

"Well, answer me this, would you be willing to relocate to a facility in Long Island?" he asked, knowing only too well she would be close enough for him to visit on a regular basis.

"I would be willing to do whatever it takes to have this once in a lifetime opportunity."

"Good, then I'll make the arrangements. You tie up loose ends here. I have a piece of property in mind, it's on the seashore. You know you'll need a lab assistant. I'd like to recommend Thomas Sheffield, if we can get him and his new bride to move to New York. He worked with my father. Dad had a lot of confidence in him and more importantly he kept his secret. I'll arrange for a meeting, if you're interested." She silently agreed.

The following morning Jonathan caught a flight home and returned to his office in Manhattan; he immediately employed the services of an architect to begin designs on the new lab. He owned a large piece of property near the Hamptons located on the northern side of the island. It was private, secluded, and faced the Atlantic Ocean.

Some weeks later Marian flew to New York to assist the architect in designing the building that would include living quarters. She wasn't exactly sure what all she needed and even though she knew money was no object, she remained frugal. Having never visited Long Island she enjoyed the sandy white beaches and towering sand dunes; not to mention the tranquility of the sea. The Hamptons had been named the sixth wealthiest area in the nation and, best of all, it was just east of Manhattan. Security was very important and the lab was outfitted with a state of the art security system and video surveillance. The blueprints were completed and approved, and construction began. It would take a total of six months to erect the building and three more months to finish the inside. All said and done, it took over ten million dollars to get the lab up and running.

Marian continued her work at the university and would occasionally fly to Long Island to see Jonathan and inspect the progress of the lab. Over those many months they spent a lot of time together. They realized there was something more between them other than just the professor's work. During her last visit she asked Jonathan about the lab assistant he recommended and arrangements were made for a meeting.

Back in Chiptaw, Thomas and Telesa were enjoying their wedded bliss and both had moved into her apartment. It seemed strange to everyone that if they had two million dollars between them why they hadn't bought a home? They paid off their debts and donated a portion of the money to several different charities.

Telesa took time off work to spend all her days and nights with Thomas. *They must be-a truly in love*, thought Papa and Mama *because they spend-a so much time together.* Well, the fact is Thomas was getting a little restless.

Midnight enjoyed being just a plain old house cat. He spent most of his days lying in the sun, lapping up saucers of milk and discovering more about his powers. Not only could he appear and disappear, but he could heal the sick and converse telepathically with whomever he chose. But something else happening, that he didn't understand.

Sitting on the dining room table looking at Thomas, his collar radiated light each time he sent a message. *"Thomas, I still have this deep desire to return home, but where is home? Something else is going on that I don't understand. Can you help me?"*

Telesa walked in and saw the two of them staring at

one another. "What can I do to help you little guy?" She stood motionless, watched and listened. *"I need you to go to New York and work with Professor Rutherford. You are my only chance to return home. You have to help the professor."*

Telesa couldn't stand the suspense any longer. She said in jest, "All right, are you guys talking about me?" Midnight turned and flaunted his eyes as she petted his head and stroked his lanky body. She saw his collar light up again and heard, *"Thomas, it's time to tell her."*

"It's time to tell me what?" she asked. Thomas sat her down, took her hand and tried to explain from the beginning. She stopped him and said, "I know, Thomas. You don't have to say anything. I remember everything that happened that night. I know Midnight healed me. I was afraid to say anything."

He held her in his arms and asked, "But why honey?" She said, "I'm just glad to be alive and if Midnight needs our help, then what are we waiting for?"

"Even if it means leaving Chiptaw?" he asked. The phone rang and it was Jonathan who invited them for a visit. Telesa agreed and they were on the next flight to New York. Of course the cat came along too, but he provided his own transportation.

Chapter 12

This was the first time Telesa had ever flown on a commercial jet. She was so excited and Thomas was elated. Arriving late in the afternoon, Jonathan met them at the airport and escorted them to The Hamptons; after giving them a brief tour of the island. Telesa, having never ventured out of Chiptaw, was thrilled with all the sights and sounds. She never dreamed she would actually see New York and visit a place she had only read about. It was so very different from Chiptaw. She was used to towering mountains and a population of only a couple thousand and here, on this one hundred and twenty five mile island, the population was well over a million.

Before meeting Marian at the restaurant, Jonathan asked to speak to Thomas alone. They left Telesa sitting in the lounge with a glass of wine. "Honey, we'll be right back," he assured her as he followed Jonathan outside.

"Thomas, how is Midnight? Did you bring him along?"

"Oh, I'm sure he's around here somewhere."

"Thomas I don't know what it is about that cat but when I read my father's notes he mentioned something about a lab accident involving a cat. Was it Midnight?"

"It was."

"I knew it. I have to tell you something and I hope you'll believe me, but that cat healed me. I don't know how, but after he placed his paws on me, I woke up the next morning and I was cured of Parkinson's. My doctor's are dumbfounded. There's no other explanation. And we saw him heal Telesa. How does he do it?"

"I don't know, Jonathan. Ever since he was a kitten he's been very special. I kept trying to tell the professor he could talk, just little words at first, but I don't think he ever believed me. But after the transformation, I think he started to realize I was telling the truth. There's always been something unique about that cat even before the lab accident."

Jonathan let out a deep sigh and said, "Thomas, Professor Rutherford has read Dad's notes and she wants to carry on his research, but she's having a few problems accepting our mystical little friend. Midnight came to me and asked me to help him return home by getting Marian, I mean Professor Rutherford to take over Dad's work. It's the least I can do after he's given me a second chance at life. So, here we are in Long Island where we're building a state of the art facility and I hope you'll seriously consider coming to work here."

They went inside where Marian was waiting and Jonathan made the appropriate introductions. They were seated when discussions ensued about employing Thomas as the professor's lab assistant; each time Thomas would glance across the table at Telesa studying her reaction. The conversation turned to Midnight when Thomas asked, "Professor, if I consider coming to work for you, do you have a problem with me bringing my cat?"

Marian knew she was being set up. "Oh you mean the magical one?" At that moment Midnight appeared in the center of the table facing the professor. She stared through him being careful not to acknowledge his presence. Of course everyone else could see the furry little feline.

As his collar glowed, all eyes were upon him. The silence was broken as Midnight uttered his first spoken words, "*I am a creation of science and I need your help. I have special powers I can't explain. I am destined to help those in need but, my desire to return home overpowers me. Please help me professor.*"

She was speechless. She heard him speak with her very own ears and so did everyone else. Jonathan described how Midnight cured his Parkinson's and Telesa told her story. Thomas said, "It was Midnight who got Jonathan to contact you about carrying on the professor's work." She pulled her chair closer to the table and extended the palm of her hand touching the cat gently on the nose. He purred and fluttered his eyes as she stroked his head and back.

"You are real aren't you?" she asked.

Jonathan smiled and said, "He's real Marian, and you

are the key to helping him just as he has helped us. Won't you please try?"

She paused and answered, "Yes, but Thomas I'll need your help."

"No problem," said the new lab assistant as he looked at Telesa for confirmation. The waiter entered and the cat vanished. Dinner was ordered and Thomas asked for a small petite steak, medium rare for Midnight.

The next day Thomas and Telesa returned to Virginia and made plans to move to Long Island. She always said she would never leave Chiptaw but she loved Thomas and Midnight so much, how could she deny them this chance of a lifetime?

It wasn't long before the lab was finished. It was true, money could buy anything. As far as anyone knew, this was simply a distinctly designed house sitting high on a sand dune above the Atlantic Ocean.

For the time being they stayed at the lab in the living quarters provided. Before relocating permanently from New York, Marian spent all her free time reading the professor's notes trying to understand how he was able to accomplish creating a human clone beyond the embryo stage. She had the same exact equipment, but the conditions were different. Something essential was missing.

Springtime finally arrived in Long Island. Leaves returned to the barren trees. Cardinals were getting their nest ready as squirrels taught their young the art of survival. Seagulls soared over the seashore as Mother Nature reset the balance of yet another season.

Working together the first few weeks was awkward for

Thomas and the professor. It was taking time to build a trusting relationship. They spent countless hours discussing the techniques used by Professor ReMax to try and duplicate the night the cat was transformed into a clone.

Thomas tried desperately to recall the sequence of events. “Professor, what I remember is that Midnight got into some of the chemicals a few days before, and it made him very irrational and sick. I brought him to the lab, showed him to the professor, who immediately placed him in the decompression chamber. After going through the series of lights, boom, there was Midnight, better than I had ever seen him, but he looked different. He was all black, when before he had a touch of white on his head and chest. Then we noticed the collar around his neck, which wasn’t there before, and each time he sent a telepathic message it would light up.”

Marian was befuddled, there wasn’t any scientific basis for what she was hearing. “Tell me about the chemicals Thomas,” she appealed.

“Well, other than what the professor has in his notes, I really can’t say. I recall there was a distinct odor. I asked him about it several times but he never shared that information with me. And while we’re on the subject of Midnight, I’ve always wondered about his ability to speak before the lab accident. Can you explain that Marian?”

“Are you telling me that before he was cloned, your cat could speak?”

“Yes, ma’am. I tried to talk to the professor about it but he did just what you’re doing, he didn’t believe me.”

The hours passed and Thomas was anxious to get back

to Telesa. She had been out shopping all day, buying this and that to decorate their quarters and she prepared a dinner fit for a king. As he entered, he could smell his favorite dish cooking, roast beef and potatoes. The small kitchenette was just large enough to accommodate a table for two, covered with a light blue linen cloth that matched perfectly with the shade of blue she chose for the curtains. Candles were burning and the lights were turned down low.

"Honey, I'm home," he chuckled. Midnight was sitting on the floor drinking his milk. Not getting a response he called again, "Honey?" From behind the door she appeared. She was a spectacular sight standing there wearing a most stunning dress. With a smile he said, "I must be the luckiest man alive." He took her in his arms and kissed her.

Meanwhile, Marian had an unexpected visit from Jonathan and as she opened the door he took her hand and looked in her eyes and said, "Marian, I can't keep hiding my feelings for you. I don't know what else to say."

She was not surprised and she confided, "I have feelings for you too Jonathan." They embraced and shared their first kiss.

Morning came quickly and it was back to the daily routine. Marian's day started as usual, reading the professor's voluminous notes. She came upon the section referring to the genome which was the DNA content that included all forty-four autosomes, two gender chromosomes and mitochondrial DNA. She questioned Thomas about the professor's source of DNA, only to learn that Professor ReMax was the source.

Reading on, she saw that the professor used his DNA

to map out complex traits and genetic variations, but somehow the experiment failed because all functional elements in the human genome sequence were exact except the one resulting in the fragile x-syndrome, a genetic mental deficiency. She realized this was why the clone remained in a vegetative state. But that's not what happened to Midnight. The cat was successfully cloned without a genetic mental deficiency. Instead he was cloned possessing magical powers, which was totally absurd.

She had to keep reminding herself what Professor ReMax taught her. '*Don't let your scientific intellect prevent you from accepting the impossible because the impossible is always possible.*' She kept comparing the professor's experiment with the human clone to Midnight's clone and the only difference between the two was the vat of chemicals the cat fell into days before the transformation. She decided that recreating the chemicals was the key, so they began work immediately trying to reconstruct those elements. Midnight was very much a part of the research. He was questioned over and over about the vat of chemicals. But even with his supernatural powers he couldn't provide the information they needed. Other than the smell of sulfur he couldn't contribute anything further.

They mixed several chemical components in search of the right blend, but not any of them carried that distinct odor. Finally out of sheer desperation Marian added a drop of sulfur to the mixture and Thomas identified the scent right away. "That's it professor. That's the smell. What did you do different?"

"I added a drop of sulfur. No, it can't be that simple,

can it?" she asked. They were ready to proceed to the next step but they couldn't risk harming Midnight. They needed another feline to experiment on first. Midnight appeared in the room sniffing the air recognizing the aroma but with his keen sense of smell he could tell something was still missing.

After many more months of study, Marian conceded that perhaps Midnight wasn't a clone but the result of a transformation which was the consequence of a mutation causing his DNA genetic material to change. She knew that point mutations were often caused by chemicals or malfunction of DNA replication. She tried various combinations of methylating agents and polycyclic hydrocarbons to mutate both replicating and non-replicating DNA. Nitrous acid would have definitely been one of the chemicals necessary and perhaps that's what was missing from the equation.

She read where the professor reversed the point mutation with another point mutation, which changed it back to its original state. *But, how did the transformation take place? Of course, it had to be something associated with the decompression chamber. But what was so different about the decompression chamber other than it had its own source of radiation?*

She read further and determined that ultraviolet and ionizing rays were used but they were very common, nothing unusual. Sitting back in her chair she sipped her cup of hot tea and reflected. *Radiation is thought of as energy in motion, either at speeds equal to the speed of light or speeds less than the speed of light. Velocities of molecules form along with particles of electrons, protons and neutrons, and in a state of rest these particles have mass, and are the constituents of atoms and atomic nuclei. And when these forms of matter travel at high velocities, then it's logical that they can transform a fragment of chromosomal DNA with its cloning vector. And following the introduction into a suitable host, the DNA can then be reproduced along with the host cell DNA.* "That's it, that's got to be it!" she shouted as she jotted down her theory.

The following day the experiment began. They would try and clone Midnight by taking his DNA and the saved samples from the last experiment. They would use the somatic cell nuclear transfer technology, with one exception. Instead of utilizing an egg and replacing the nucleus from a mature body cell they were going to use Midnight's DNA, and the mammary gland cell of another feline. They would then take the genome and through the process of parthenogenesis they would treat the cell with chemicals causing it to divide.

Once the division stops, which should take about five days, they would place the surviving genomes in the decompression chamber and expose them to electromagnetic radiation. This would create a wave-particle duality, and in theory be the foundation for a quantum leap. If it works they should have a clone of Midnight. Preparations were made. They were apprehensive. If successful this would be a medical breakthrough towards cloning via the mutation of a somatic cell nuclei.

The day finally arrived. The genomes finished separating and were immersed in the chemicals and this time they added the Nitrous acid. The familiar smell of sulfur was present, along with another unidentified scent, the one that had been extinct. After treating the genomes, they were placed in the decompression chamber and switches, two, three, and nine were triggered. The cascade of lights continued. First red, then green, and finally blue. Out of the blue light came a magnificent white light; so bright they were forced to look away followed by a low pulsating hum, piercing screech and high pitched ring. Then, the rotation of lights ended and everything stopped. The smell of sulfur was increasingly strong and coming from the chamber.

With great anticipation they opened the chamber and inside they saw an adult feline alive and well. "This is incredible," shouted the professor as she removed the all white cat from the chamber and placed him on the table. She listened as she took his vitals, moving the stethoscope over his entire body. She looked at Thomas as he said to her, "There's not a heartbeat is there professor?"

"No, yet the animal is alive and breathing. I can hear his lungs and all his organs working but he has no heart beat. How can that be?" she asked.

"I don't know, but it was the same way before." Midnight became visible on the table next to the cat that appeared to be about his size and shape, except he was solid white. He wore the same clear collar, made of the same smooth material, and a strange force forbid its removal. They noticed the same silver pendant and as they inspected the pendant they witnessed the spelling out of the name, *Ghost Kitty.*

Chapter 13

Midnight tried to communicate telepathically with his feline brother but there was little reaction. Once offered food he devoured the morsels in seconds. "Well, at least he eats," said the professor. "Thomas, do you realize what we have accomplished?"

"No, professor not really. You know, something just doesn't seem right about that cat." They place the cat in a cage for the night and retire for the evening. Midnight stayed behind studying this mutation of himself with a great sense of vigilance.

When morning came the professor opened the door

to the lab and found Midnight and Ghost Kitty sitting on the table facing each other. "Midnight, did you let him out of his cage?"

"No, professor. He has the ability to disappear and reappear just like me." She was about to speak when her lab assistant entered.

"Thomas, quick, close the door," she ordered.

"Hey," he said, "I see the little guy made it through the night."

Midnight announced, *"He has some of my powers, but there's something very dark about that cat."*

Thomas laughed and said, "Oh, little buddy, you're just jealous." Ghost Kitty started to growl as Midnight took a stance daring him to fight and the growling stopped.

The professor continued to examine the white cat who had an obvious zest for food. He loved to eat and he ate plenty without even a meow to say 'Thank you.' Other than his initial growl, he made little effort to communicate. He kept quiet and watched everyone and everything. It was obvious he was studying them as much as they were observing him. He absorbed every little detail, and he learned quickly.

In the days that followed Midnight never left the lab trying to learn more about his clone and the extent of his powers. Thomas too, had reservations as he sensed something just wasn't right about that cat.

As time passed the brotherly felines played an endless game of cat and mouse with cat chasing cat, disappearing and reappearing. And still no communication between them, other than an occasional growl or hiss. Midnight wasn't convinced that these parlor tricks weren't the only tricks this cat dominated. There was something very corrupt about him and Midnight knew he couldn't be trusted. Other than the fact that he was all white, he was the black cat's identical twin.

Thomas tried for the first time to pet the scantly feline but the cat didn't respond. There was no purring or kneading, no reaction when his back was scratched. It was as though he hadn't any emotions. This was an interesting observation which he brought to the attention of the professor.

"Marian, you know, this was the same problem we had with the human clone. The professor felt it didn't possess a soul, because it was in a vegetative state. But this cat isn't in a vegetative state, yet, he has no emotions. Does that mean he has no soul?"

"That's been my perception as well, Thomas. I've noticed he scrutinizes everything we do and it's like he understands, but he doesn't want us to know." Thomas dangled a string in front of him trying to get his attention, but there he sat, non-responsive. Midnight appeared in the room directly behind Ghost Kitty, who without warning turned around and with a swift swat of his paw struck Midnight across the nose, grazing his whiskers. He disappeared and reappeared across the room. He started to growl and with the hump of his back invited Midnight to accept his challenge to fight. "*Well, it's about time*," said the black cat as he disappeared and reappeared across the room in front of the estranged cat. They became entangled in a large ball of fur spitting and growling. They spun around in circles with their collars illuminating when all at once, they vanished.

"Where did they go? We have to find them. If that cat escapes there's no telling what he'll do," shouted Marian. They searched the entire complex and found nothing.

Meanwhile, both Midnight and Ghost Kitty were taking quantum leaps from one dimension to the other. This chase was only the beginning. Wherever Ghost Kitty ventured, Midnight followed. Gravity and electromagnetic forces had no effect on the felines as they traveled from one dimension to the next. They were trapped in this endless cycle of cat chasing cat until finally they crashed landing back in the third dimension from whence they came.

The earth beneath them was a field of tall green grass underneath a dark blue sky somewhere in the middle of nowhere. Both were exhausted and laid down to rest. Midnight tried to communicate telepathically, no reaction. He tried speaking words, no reaction. All attempts to connect with his feline brother, fail. They regain their strength and the hissing and growling commences. Midnight knew this animal was out of control and had to be stopped.

Their encounter was interrupted by a group of young hikers. The cats were noticed as they came closer. Midnight let out a friendly "*Meow.*" Ghost Kitty however, kept his distance, focusing all his energy on one young man. His collar radiates light. This is the first time Midnight can sense his concentration, but it's too late.

The young man felt extreme pain throughout his body, lost his balance and fell, hitting his head on a jagged rock. Unconscious and bleeding profusely, his friends feared he would die, he was a hemophiliac. Midnight knew what needed to be done. He placed his paws on the young man's head, his collar glowed as heat radiated from the pads of his paws and their friend was mysteriously healed. Midnight collapses.

While everyone assembles around the extraordinary cat, Ghost Kitty disappears and Midnight is too weak to follow. He listened as the young man told his incredible story.

"I've always been protected by my parents because of my fragile condition. One minor cut could cost me my life. I don't understand how or why I've been cured, but I thank God for sending me this special little cat that came to my rescue." He didn't know why he fell; he remembered only making eye contact with the white cat and then everything going black.

The hikers wanted to take Midnight with them, but before they had the chance he vanished. He didn't go far because he was still too weak. He rested beneath a red maple in a pile of dried leaves as darkness fell upon the earth.

As time passed he regained his strength. The sensitive whiskers around his mouth worked like radar and assisted him in detecting the whereabouts of his prey and his prey was Ghost Kitty. His erect pointed ears acted like a directional antenna and his rounded head and short muzzle acted like a receiver. His claws were withdrawn from their protective sheaths as he received pulses of electromagnetic waves. As he stood each of the five toes on his forefeet began to pulsate. His tail waved back and forth, up and down, and left to right. His sense of hearing was excellent and precise. The collar around his neck started to glow and he vanished. He was on the trail of the evil white cat.

His intuition told him he could be found meandering in a place high above where he could view the world below. Perched on top of a towering skyscraper in Manhattan sat Ghost Kitty looking down on the city. Midnight became visible behind him and introduced himself with a violent sounding growl followed by a series of swatting motions. Ghost Kitty vanished and Midnight followed.

They ended up in a most familiar place, Jonathan's law office. The sun was rising and the game of cat and mouse, with cat chasing cat, was getting tiresome. But this was just the beginning.

The building was quiet as the new dawn presented herself. As the sun rose, rays of light radiated against the sides of the tall concrete structures, and the streets were already busy as this was a city that never sleeps.

Midnight now knew Ghost Kitty could communicate telepathically with humanoids. He also knew he could make humanoids do and say things they didn't want to, and in turn harm themselves or others. He had to be stopped but how? His powers were equal to his own.

Midnight tried again to converse telepathically with his brother. "*What is it you want?*" Finally he got an answer, but not the one he expected.

"*I am you. I am the dark side of you. I do what you cannot. Humanoids are our enemies. They are cruel and tried to kill us when we were only kittens. But, you, why do you protect those who tried to do us harm?*"

Midnight, horrified by his response, did everything he

could to reason with him. "*Not all humanoids are bad. Look at Thomas who saved us from the freezing cold when he pulled us out of that dumpster. And what about Telesa and Professor Rutherford who cloned you?*" Ghost Kitty did not want to listen. He was adamant that his destiny was to seek and destroy all humanoids.

As nine o'clock approached Jonathan entered his office and saw not one but two cats sitting on top of his desk with papers spread all across the floor. He could sense the tension in the room. He asked, "What's going on Midnight and who's your friend?"

"*Be careful Jonathan. This cat is here to hurt you.*" He didn't need any further explanation. He turned to walk away as Ghost Kitty focused on his thoughts. The cat's collars begin to glow; it was a battle between good and evil. Suddenly a fire ignites the curtains and spreads quickly to the sofa. Midnight suspends Jonathan in the air to keep him away from the flames. But the flames grow higher. The cat has to release his grip in order to extinguish the fire. Jonathan falls and crawls to the nearby door, it slams shut. He chokes and coughs from the thick smoke and cries, "Midnight, I can't breathe."

After dousing the flames to less than a flicker the black cat came to the aid of his friend who was barely breathing. He placed his paws on Jonathan's chest and as his collar illuminated, Ghost Kitty vanished. His breathing was shallow, he wasn't getting enough oxygen. His power to heal wasn't working. *Why can't I heal him like before*? He had to get help or Jonathan would die. Using his powers of telepathy, firemen from unit sixty four arrived and started hitting the door with an ax; the door flew open. They give Jonathan oxygen; he regains consciousness and starts to breathe again. Knowing his friend was safe Midnight departed and realized that once he healed someone, he could never heal them again.

The search for his evil clone was more important then ever. Utilizing the whiskers around his mouth he sniffed the air and turned his head left to right. His ears were erect as he moved his tail back and forth. Each of the five toes on his forefeet began to pulsate. The collar around his neck glowed brightly. His destination was determined and in the blink of an eye he vanished and reappeared in Chiptaw. The apartment where he stayed with Thomas and Telesa was empty without them, but there were signs that Ghost Kitty had been there and not very long ago.

Midnight continued to follow his trail and found himself at Papa and Mama's, but he was too late. He could sense something was terribly wrong as he lingered. It was clear that Papa and Mama had been abducted but, he had no sense of their whereabouts. His extrasensory perception was blocked.

But with his keen sense of hearing he heard knocking from beneath the wooden floor. He followed the noise to the kitchen where the sound grew louder. He found the door to the cellar and realized Papa and Mama were trapped inside. Using his powers he lifted the door and tossed it across the room along with its hinges. He heard running water and faint cries for help. Papa and Mama were almost fully submerged with only their noses barely above the surface. He had to do something, and he had to do it fast, or they would drown. He used his powers of levitation to try and raise them, but they were restrained.

He swam to where their hands were tied together and their feet chained to a metal pole. He freed them just as the water covered them fully. Papa swam to the surface taking a breath. Seeing that Mama was still trapped below, he swam down to get her. She stopped breathing. Papa brought her to the surface, pulled her out of the cellar, and cried as he held her in his arms.

"Oh Mama, do not-a leave me. Papa he-a needs you. Mama, do not-a leave me." Midnight crawled out and placed his paws on her chest. His collar glows as Papa watches and sees Mama start to breathe. "Oh, Mama, you did not-a leave me," cried Papa. "Where am I? What's-a goin' on?" She saw Midnight and said, "Papa it's-a Midnight. Help me get up. I got-a get-a him some milk. He's Mama's special little boy." The brave little cat collapses, Papa wraps him in a warm towel and takes him home. When morning came, Midnight was gone.

His journey takes him to the lab where it is peaceful and quiet, but the stillness is soon plagued by the attack of the malicious white cat. Strong, sharp, curved claws were drawn with each stalking the other. Their canine teeth with sharp cutting edges, were revealed as each growled and hissed. Their fighting like domestic cats wasn't going to accomplish anything as neither could be destroyed. They were invincible.

They were aloof and independent with one good and one evil, yet things were not in balance. "*Where are they?*" demanded Midnight. Ghost Kitty refused to answer and kept stalking the black cat. *"I know you've done something with them. Tell me where they are."*

Ghost Kitty was not a vocal fur ball when it came to communicating. He was silent and withdrawn and didn't even act like a cat. But he wasn't just a cat. He had special powers and he meant to do harm to those who harmed him. He stalked his victims with great stealth and diligence, making them do things they didn't want to do, like locking themselves inside the decompression chamber.

Realizing their location, Midnight attempted to open the heavy steel doors using all his strength, but he couldn't and as he turned to look for the evil cat he heard the triggering of switches two, three, and nine. The chamber began its series of rotating lights. He tried desperately to send Thomas a message. *"If you can hear me you must open the door from inside. You are in danger."* Jumping over to the control panel, Midnight disengaged the switches and the rotation of lights stopped, and the heavy steel door opened and out stepped two very confused humans.

Ghost Kitty leaps and lands between Midnight and the two humanoids, and taking a stance he speaks his first words, *"All humans must be annihilated. Don't you remember what the shadow people did to us? They're everywhere and they are here to defeat us. They must be destroyed."*

Ghost Kitty turns and faces the two very frightened humans and as his golden eyes turn red, the collar around his neck glows. The professor is getting very hot but the temperature in the room stays the same. Suddenly, without provocation, the professor burst into flames driven by an inner storm. Within seconds fire erupts furiously from her chest engulfing her head and igniting her hair, turning her into a human torch.

She screams in agony. Midnight pounces on top of her putting out the flames. He places his paws on her badly burned body as the violent wounds turn to simple burns and blisters. She is healed and Midnight collapses while Ghost Kitty makes his escape.

Chapter 14

This game of cat and mouse with cat hunting cat grew very tiresome. Midnight could endlessly chase the evil cat, cleaning up all the messes he leaves behind, or find a way to destroy him. Since science created this monster, then science should be the answer to his destruction.

So, work began immediately to find a solution. It was decided they would set a trap using a mouse; something all felines fancied. Even though Ghost Kitty had special powers, he was still a cat and cats love mice. They discussed the pros and cons of creating a mutant cloned mouse.

There were many things to consider. First they had

to come up with some sort of chemical combination that could destroy Ghost Kitty. Secondly, they had to determine what went wrong with the last experiment because they certainly didn't want to create another evil mutant clone. After much debate the decision was made.

There were many failed attempts. The professor mixed methylating agents with polycyclic hydrocarbons, nitrous acid, and a touch of sulfur, which was the previous recipe; but this time she also added adysic acid, hydrochloride, and activated carbons counteracting the polycyclic hydrocarbons minimally. This changed the chemical variation enough that it made it possible to have control over the mutant cloned mouse. But, the only way to tell if it was going to work was to expose Midnight. If successful, he would temporarily become incapacitated.

Everything was in place and the experiment proceeded with every possible precaution. Midnight was exposed to the raw chemicals and, as expected, he became sick. Within two hours he was back to his old self without any ill effects, and he still had his powers. The goal was to introduce the chemicals into the mutant mouse and to use him as bait to destroy Ghost Kitty. Midnight would have to keep his distance for his own protection.

The process began using somatic cell nuclear transfer technology. They took the DNA of an ordinary house mouse and the mammary gland cell of an American white footed mouse and treated the cells with the first set of chemicals. They then took the genomes through the parthenogenesis process causing them to divide. Once completed, the surviving genomes were placed in the decompression chamber and exposed to electromagnetic radiation, after being immersed in the second set of chemicals. Switches two, three, and nine were triggered followed by the rotation of lights. Then came a low pulsating hum followed by a piercing screech and a high pitched ring. The procedure was complete but did it work?

They opened the door and there laid a little grey mouse with a touch of white on each paw and the same clear collar around his neck. The creature was lifeless and not breathing. The professor placed him on the table. She didn't expect a heartbeat, but she did expect him to be breathing.

"It must have been the second dose of chemicals. Perhaps it was just too much," she said. A reluctant Midnight came near and placed his short muzzle against the mouth of the rodent. With one deep breath, he blew air into the lungs of the lifeless body and the little mouse started to breathe. The thin, clear collar around his neck started to glow as the cat stepped back, keeping his distance.

"The mission now is to determine the extent of his powers," said Midnight who didn't seem to be experiencing any ill effects.

"That's very interesting," said the professor.

"What?" asked Thomas.

"The cat wasn't affected after having direct contact with the mouse. I'm concerned now if we used the proper level of chemicals."

Midnight cautiously approached and inspected the mouse that looked like a normal grey mouse, alert and sniffing his nose in the air. He took his course tongue and groomed the tiny mouse who responded by licking the cat on the head.

Cheese was introduced for the first time and he consumed it by holding the small piece in his front paws and sitting on his backside, taking small bites as he gorged himself. The professor continued her observations while stroking the body of the little rodent. She said "It's as though he has bonded with you, Midnight. Perhaps he doesn't want to harm you. There's no way to tell until we can learn more about him."

Midnight started to teach him the differences between good and evil. Lessons on how to disappear and reappear were mimicked perfectly by the little mouse. They did this over and over again in the confines of the lab and each time the mouse was successful.

Next, Midnight started levitating small items like test tubes of different sizes and shapes which were also mimicked by the mouse, with one or two broken incidents. The cat chuckled, "*Yes, you need a little more work with your levitation powers.*"

The final test of telepathy was attempted as the black cat focused on the mouse. All of a sudden the little mouse jumped up and ran across the room and hid in the corner. He was afraid. As the cat went over to him, the rodent extended his pointed snout, wiggled his small ears, and shook his hairless tail. He stretched his elongated slender body towards his natural predator, the cat.

"*Its okay little guy, I'm your friend and I will not harm you. I think we'll call you Roedee Rodent. So come on Roedee, we've got work to do and you needn't be afraid.*"

They spent all their time together playing and having fun, but also teaching and learning. The little mouse was like a sponge, soaking up any and all information and with that knowledge he became very strong and powerful. He not only learned how to communicate telepathically, but he learned to speak as well, and he was always asking questions.

"*Midnight, where did I come from and how did we become friends, when we're supposed to be natural enemies?*" asked the nervous little mouse.

The cat replied, "*The professor cloned you just like I was cloned, but you didn't make it through the cycle of lights.*"

Roedee didn't understand and asked, "*What is the cycle of lights?*"

Midnight started to growl, letting his little friend know he was asking far too many questions and the mouse reacted. He stood up on his hind legs and sniffed the air with his pointed nose, and as his collar glowed the cat took a step backwards, laid down and remained still for almost two hours. The little mouse was frantic, not realizing what he had done. He layed down next to the sickly feline and waited. Once recovered, Midnight decided it was time for them to have a cat and mouse talk.

"*Roedee, you must listen to me very carefully. But before I tell you what I'm about to tell you, it's important that you know we are friends, even though nature has made us natural enemies. But not all cats will be your friends. You were not breathing after going through the cycle of lights so I breathed life into you and you were born.*" The little mouse listened intently as the cat continued.

"You were created for the sole purpose to defeat a cat named, Ghost Kitty. He is a very evil cat and his only objective is to destroy all humans; he must be stopped. Do you understand?" Roedee wiggled his ears and nodded his head. *"You were given this gift by the professor to be used only against evil. Do you understand?"*

Roedee asked, *"Is that what I did to you when you growled at me?"* Midnight answered with the nod of his head. *"You need to learn to control that power and use it only against evil,"* exclaimed Midnight as he vanished. Roedee did not follow his friend because he didn't know he could. He sat and pondered what he had just learned.

Meantime, Midnight met with Marian and Thomas and explained what happened. The professor petted him on the head to reassure him that they were doing the right thing. "You know Midnight, you and that mouse," and she was interrupted.

"His name is Roedee," said the agitated feline.

"Of course, well, you and Roedee seem to have a connection that you and Ghost Kitty don't have. It may have something to do with you breathing life into him, but the both of you are definitely connected. Do you think you can trust him to help you now that he knows about his special gifts?"

He lowered his head and said, *"I sure hope so."*

Thomas picked up his cat, hugged him and said, "Its all right little man, everything will be all right."

Midnight purrs, raises his head and says, *"Well, there's one sure way to find out,"* and he vanished.

Many days pass before he returns. The professor and her lab assistant spend hours each day, teaching the little mouse the difference between good and evil and right from wrong. And they especially teach him about loyalty to his special gift.

Midnight reappears across the room, staring at Roedee, who jumps up and down with excitement and runs towards him. Roedee's collar starts to glow as Midnight takes a step backwards.

"Don't worry Midnight. I've been practicing my powers and I've got them under control. I'm ready to go after that evil cat." At that very exact moment they touched noses and vanished. The hunt for Ghost Kitty had begun.

Their quest seemed to never end. They stopped often, Roedee couldn't keep up with bouncing back and forth between dimensions so Midnight questioned if his little friend was up to confronting evil, thinking he was in need of more practice.

But, all at once Midnight's whiskers detected a vibration as his pointed ears stood erect. He withdrew his claws and waited. Ghost Kitty appeared and sneered, *"Looks like I'm just in time for dinner."* Roedee didn't appreciate that remark one bit.

"I'm not your dinner butthead, I'm your terminator," he said. The evil cat laughed as he leapt towards the mouse grabbing him in his mouth, holding him tightly between his long canine teeth.

Midnight disappeared while the collar around Roedee's neck started to glow. Within seconds the evil cat dropped his prey and fell to the ground trapped inside his paralyzed body with his powers useless. He had no idea what happened.

Midnight reappeared and stood over him making sure

he couldn't escape. He was totally incapacitated, but not for long. While in his captive state Midnight tried to reason with him. "*You must change your evil ways or be done away with cat, not all humanoids are wicked. You have destined yourself to annihilate the entire human population and there is no need. We are domestic creatures and we need them as much as they need us,*" preached the black cat, but his words were wasted.

As he lay there quiet and still, Roedee moved towards him, sniffing the air with his pointed snout. Sitting down next to Midnight he asked, "*Do I finish the job?*" At that moment Ghost Kitty moved his eyes. He was coming out of the stillness and a decision had to be made.

The black cat demanded, "*Well, what's it going to be? You're either with us or against us. This will be your only chance. Make up your mind now.*"

The evil white cat remained still even though he was fully recovered. He was planning his escape. Roedee, being the inquisitive little mouse he was, asked, "*Midnight, why are you trying to help him? I thought I was here to put an end to him? Now let's get rid of this dirtball.*"

Ghost Kitty closed his eyes to rest when suddenly he vanished. The chase was on again. Good against evil; two against one. But this time, Ghost Kitty was aware of Roedee's purpose and it was going to be much harder to catch him. But what he didn't know is that the mouse had the same affect on Midnight. There was no doubt Roedee could do what he was designed to do and hence, Midnight's fears were put to rest.

They made quantum leaps from one dimension to the next in search of the evil cat. It became a game for Roedee, chasing his natural enemy instead of being chased. How powerful this made him feel, but seeking out his prey wasn't easy. He had to depend on Midnight's keen senses as his senses were nothing compared to that of the *Cats.*

Their trek brought them to an alley in another big city. It was dark and smelled of rotting garbage. A cat sitting on a fence catches a glimpse of the little mouse and in one fleeting moment, captures him in his mouth and commences chomping down on the not so tasty mouse. Roedee struggles to get free but he's trapped by the cat's paws around his body. His collar glows but nothing happens.

"Hey," yells Roedee. *"Let go of me birdbrain, or I'll clobber you."* Then after a couple more bites the cat surprisingly spit him out along with a slimy fur ball. *"Oh, man, this is so gross,"* shouts Roedee as he watches the cat clean the stench off his face and paws.

Midnight approaches the little mouse with caution and sees his left shoulder has been bitten. He's about to heal him when all of a sudden the gash on his shoulder fades away. *"Wow, Roedee how did you do that?"* asked Midnight. The little mouse was so traumatized he didn't even realize he'd healed himself.

"How did I do what?" he asked.

"You fixed your shoulder. Don't you remember?"

Looking frazzled he turned to Midnight and said, *"The only thing I remember is that cat chomping down on me. Why didn't he get sick? I should have been able to make my first kill. What did I do wrong?"*

Midnight took a seat next to his troubled little friend

and said, "*Calm down. You didn't do anything wrong. Your powers have no affect on regular cats, only me and Ghost Kitty.*"

Wiggling his tail he asked, "*You mean that cat could have eaten me and there isn't anything I could have done about it?*"

Midnight snickered and said, "*Well, it looked to me like you didn't taste so good. Besides what do you have to worry about? You can heal yourself.*" This had indeed been a lesson learning day for Roedee, who failed to realize, he always had the power to escape. All he had to do was disappear.

Chapter 15

Their next destination was the suburbs of Hartford, Connecticut. It was springtime, the essence of Mother Nature's beauty was exasperating with the manicured lawns, endless green landscaping, and fluffy white clouds. Birds were singing and squirrels were chasing each other up and down the tall maples hiding behind their large new born leaves.

"*What brings us here?*" asked Roedee.

Midnight sniffed the air and said, "*Ghost Kitty.*" His keen senses told him the evil cat was nearby, and his in'tuition told him there was plenty of trouble.

Meanwhile Ghost Kitty found himself sitting in a field

watching children play. A car with the keys inside was parked nearby and left unattended. Ghost Kitty focused all his energy on the thirteen year old teenager who wore a bright red buzz cut. The kid walked around the car several times and noticed the keys inside. He was naturally mischievous and welcomed this opportunity to have some fun. He looked around and the coast was clear so he jumped in the front seat of the Pontiac, started it up, stepped on the gas and ploughed into the field. He had never driven a car before except in the video games he played. He thought, *how hard could this be?*

Passerby's saw the car being driven by a kid panicked and called the police. Sounds of sirens were heard in the distance as the kid floored the accelerator to build up speed. His target was to jump the sand dune just ahead and reaching the top he went airborne and the car flipped and rolled landing upside down. The kid inside crawled out with only minor scratches. But, the cries of the three year old boy, who had been struck down, echoed faintly beneath the rubble.

There he lay near death, as Midnight and Roedee reach the outskirts of town. People were standing around looking at the boy, who was almost lifeless. Midnight forces his way through the crowd, places his paws on the small boy's chest. His collar glows, the little boy regains consciousness and he is healed. The cat collapses.

People can't believe the miracle. Roedee tries to revive his friend but he isn't strong enough, and his presence startles the crowd. He had to leave. He spots Ghost Kitty sitting close by gloating over the misery he'd caused.

Roedee vanishes and reappears next to him and screams, *"You better run cat, because I'm here to make mince-meat out of you."* A hiss follows, and a deep growl as the thin clear collar around Roedee's neck glows. The cat vanishes and the little mouse follows.

The police arrived and identified the boy driving the stolen car as Christopher ReMax, great-grandson of the professor. He was immediately arrested and his parents were contacted to meet him at the police station. It was decided the little boy suffered a fractured sternum, causing internal bleeding, but the boy miraculously recovered. The doctors were stunned and had no explanation.

Christopher tried to explain about the cat that healed the little boy, so he shouldn't get into trouble. But his story was absurd. "Young man, you're lucky to be alive," said his father in a strong parental voice. "You stole a car and you wrecked it, and you could have killed someone, not to mention yourself."

Christopher continued to interrupt, "But Dad, the kid is all right because the cat helped him, so what did I do that was so wrong?"

With an angry expression on his face he looked at his son and said, "I don't want to hear anything more about that cat, and furthermore, you're grounded for life."

Meanwhile a young woman in the crowd wrapped Midnight in a baby blanket and took him home. He was cold and tired. She knew there was something very special about this cat. She wanted to do anything she could to help him, like she saw him help the little boy. She offered him food, but he was too weary to eat. After resting several hours, he graciously accepted the food and vanished.

During the long spring night Roedee did all he could to keep up with the evil feline, but the cat was too smart and too fast and he escaped. Roedee was all alone for the very first time and he was frightened, especially now that he knew he could be eaten by *Cats.* Keeping a low profile he waited for his feline friend to find him and Midnight did just that when he materialized right next to the little mouse.

"*Midnight, you're here. I've been so afraid. Are you all right now?*" he asked.

"*Yes, but we have work to do, so let's get started.*" Once again they took quantum leaps from one dimension to the other searching for the evil cat. They stopped to rest. "*Are we ever going to catch that cat?*" asked Roedee. "*And what happens to me after he's destroyed?*"

"*I don't know. I guess you'll stay with me until we can find our way home.*"

Roedee had no idea what he was talking about. He never had a previous life. His existence was as it is today and he had nothing else to compare. He had no other life he could remember. Midnight was his only friend and they were connected in a way that made them like brothers. He was Roedee's mentor and he taught him everything he knew and they had a special bond. A bond that could not be broken, or could it?

The chase resumed. Good against evil; two against one. This time they landed in a most beautiful place, Niagara Falls. It was an awesome sight, seeing the mighty river plunge over the cliffs of dolostone and shale, and to hear the tremendous sound of rushing water cascading over the falls, creating a circle of boiling white water at its base. Where one hundred and fifty thousand gallons of liquid per second rushes over the edge and tumbles seventy feet onto the rocks below. The world knew very few who went over the falls, and survived.

Amanda Renee and her Mother, Tasha Marie, the Belle's of Society, were celebrating Amanda's new found status as one of Boston's socialites, by taking a boat ride on the Niagara River. The natural beauty of the falls and the amount of water being siphoned away was most impressive. The upper Niagara River extended twenty two miles from Lake Erie. Amanda Renee, wearing a brightly colored orange life jacket, stood on the side of the boat as water sprayed in her face, thinking about her future and who she would one day marry.

Ghost Kitty appears and fixes his sights on the charming young girl. The collar around his neck begins to glow. Tasha Marie glances over at the cat when suddenly, Amanda plummets into the icy water as Ghost Kitty vanishes. "Help, help!" she cries. "My daughter, my daughter, she's fallen overboard. Somebody please save my baby." Her heart pounds with a fear like she had never known.

The Niagara River was reaching its ninety degree turn known as the whirlpool rapids, which captured the limber body of the young girl and carried her further down the river towards the falls. The captain was alerted. He called for help on the radio. Within minutes a helicopter was in the air scanning the water for the lost teen. The boat was swiftly approaching the point of no return and had to turn back.

Tasha realized the change in direction and shouted, "No, no, you can't leave, we must find her." She was so distraught she tried to climb over the rail as several passengers restrained her. When the boat reached the shore, she climbed out and ran towards the falls. A heavy wire, already secured from each bank, was the girl's last chance to be saved. Men climbed in the water, on each side, and waited.

The river was cold and vicious. They searched for a glimpse of the bright orange life jacket. Finally they caught sight of her as each man in the water tried to judge her direction. Seconds seemed like hours as she came closer bobbing up and down in the raging water.

A hundred thousand gallons rushed down the river and the closer it came to the edge of the falls, the greater the pressure. The men could barely hang on. As the young girl came towards them, their huge hands reached out to catch her, only to miss her by mere inches. There was no hope of saving her now as the crowd watched in horror.

Midnight was positioned on the American side with Roedee hiding just beneath his belly. As she floats nearer to the rim Midnight's collar radiates a bright light. Using his powers of levitation he tries to raise her out of the water, but the force is too strong, even with the help of Roedee. In their last desperate attempt to save her they keep her elevated just above the surface as she rides down the outside of the falls. A tour boat at the base waited. "There she is," cried the first mate as people on board watched in disbelief. Three thousand tons of water crashed over the falls with the young girl riding it down landing safety away from the rocks. *But did she survive?* The boat was placed in gear and she soon came within their reach.

The crew pulled her from the freezing river. She wasn't breathing. Midnight appeared on the boat as crew members tried to revive her. She still wasn't breathing. The cat places his paws on her chest as his collar glows. Within minutes the color returns to her face and she starts to breathe. The cat collapses next to her.

The first mate, after witnessing such a miracle, wraps Midnight in his jacket as the boat returns to shore. He knew this cat had special powers and he planned to become a very rich man.

As the boat made landfall, Tasha cried as she saw Amanda wrapped in a blanket alive and well. Running into each others arms they shared a hug like they had never shared before. As the first mate disembarked the tour boat, carrying the black cat, Amanda started crying, "Mama, the cat, he saved me. You have to help him, he saved me." Amanda refused to leave without the cat. Tasha looked at the man and saw Midnight. She said, "Listen mister, you have to give him to me, he's very special."

He pulled away and said, "No way lady, I know how special he is and he's coming with me; he's going to make me very rich." Amanda kept crying with her arms outstretched followed by a temper tantrum. Tasha stood by and watched her not so aristocratic daughter scream and shout, telling everyone how this horrible man was trying to steal her beloved pet. Out of pure embarrassment the first mate handed him over and left in a huff. They returned to their hotel, where the cat rested.

Amanda couldn't stop petting him. She always wanted a cat of her very own, which her Mother would never allow, because they were animals. "But, Mother, why can't I have this cat? You know he saved me," she pleaded. At that moment Midnight made eye contact with Tasha and sent her a telepathic message.

"Tasha, I am a part of your father and I am trying to return home. There is an evil cat that I must seek out and defeat. He too is a part of your father but he is very evil and wants to destroy all humans."

Puzzled, Tasha asked, "Is it the same cat I saw on the boat?" The cat nodded his head.

She understood completely and gave Amanda her final answer, "No, you cannot have this cat or any other cat," and Midnight vanished.

A couple days passed before he caught up with Roedee. When he did, he noticed how different he looked, so he asked, *"Roedee what's up with the fur? You're all white now just like Ghost Kitty."* Roedee placed himself in front of a broken piece of glass. Looking at his reflection he noticed that his thin grey coat had turned fluffy white.

"Terrific, I look just like an oversized cotton ball," he shouted. *"Hey, what's going on here? That's just great. With this fur it's going to be real easy for the cats to find me. What's happening Midnight? What am I going to do?"*

Looking at his distressed little friend he said, *"Don't*

worry, we'll think of something. It'll be all right," and off they went into the night.

Meanwhile Ghost Kitty is preparing his own line of defense against the bizarre little mouse when he finds himself in a dark alley surrounded by a group of mean and nasty alley cats, whose only purpose is to control their territory. This group of felines shared a common identity simply by their association with one another which provided them with a sense of belonging. Everyone knew protection was in numbers and the more the cats the more the protection.

The leader of this so called gang was *Killer* and he was as street smart as they came. He feared nothing. His growl was like that of a lion, he frightened many. It was known that if anyone crossed him they would be killed. The group of cats closes in on Ghost Kitty as the collar around his neck glows.

Killer growls at the strange white cat threatening harm if he doesn't get off his turf while other members of his gang stand boldly by ready to defend their leader.

Unexpectedly, Killer is levitated in the air, swatting his paws, spitting and growling as members of his gang watch him trying to free himself from something not even there. They laugh as the leader of the pack loses all proof of his worthiness. They turn their backs and walk away.

Ghost Kitty follows, sending each of them a telepathic message. "*I'm now your leader and you will do as I say or I will destroy you.*" They stop, turn and stare at the mysterious white cat. Obviously they needed more convincing. The grip on *Killer* was released and he fell to the ground using his tail as a rudder landing on all four paws. Furious, he knew he had to prove his bravery and strength but, his brutality would only get him into trouble. He was a true predator and his instinct was to hunt and kill. With ears drawn back, his body positioned to attack he takes his last leap.

Ghost Kitty's eyes turn red as *Killer* burst into flames. The alley cat is swallowed by a ball of fire and within seconds he turns to dust and disappears in the wind. Ghost Kitty vanishes and reappears at the entrance of the alley where he is met by the fleeing felines. "*Like I said, I'm your master now and you will obey me or I will kill you.*" The frightened cats accepted their new leader and any plans to be defiant were put to rest.

At that instant Midnight and Roedee appeared with the gang of cats between them and Ghost Kitty. This made Roedee very nervous.

"*Oh, oh,*" he said as the group of cats turned, catching a glimpse of him.

Ghost Kitty hollered, "*Hey, Roedee. You look different. What happened? You look like you've seen a Ghost,*" laughed the evil white cat.

"*Yeah, well, don't get too relaxed cat because I'm going to jerk a knot in your tail so tight you'll never get away.*" Roedee knew only too well that these alley *cats* would not pass up a chance to chase a mouse that crosses their path. As they lunge towards him he disappears, leaving them sniffing the air trying to find his scent. An awful scent but nevertheless, they were hungry.

He reappears next to Ghost Kitty as the collar around his neck glows. The evil cat took a step backwards. But, Roedee had a problem; he couldn't disappear while his collar was engaged so he was a sitting target. The cats were getting close. He released his collar to escape and he vanished. It was then Ghost Kitty learned the weakness of the little mouse.

Midnight stayed behind and challenged the evil cat, even though he knew their powers were equal and nothing would be accomplished. The gang of cats surrounded Midnight who wasn't the least bit threatened. He just faded away.

The mischievous gang of cats obeyed every command of their great white leader. They were patient and they waited in the alley for hours for the little mouse to return. But, their hunger grew and the dumpsters had already been emptied by the city.

Ghost Kitty strolled out of the alley with his gang of cats following behind. They came upon a restaurant that served only the best sirloin steaks. He told his gang to wait outside. He vanished and reappeared in the kitchen.

Being spotted by the chef who was preparing a tray of filet mignon, he commenced screaming at the cat, chased him through the kitchen, out the back door, tripped and dropped the choice cuts of meat all over the ground. The gang of hungry cats attacked and dragged off their scrumptious dinner. They praised their new found leader and for the moment they were satisfied.

Little Roedee was afraid and frustrated as he thought about his future. Sitting next to Midnight he asks, "*What's going to come of me after I get rid of Ghost Kitty? And how am I going to get to him with all those cats around? Will I ever be safe? I know why I'm here, but I must have another purpose, other than chasing that cat. What's going to happen to me, and will we always be friends?"*

With a look of compassion Midnight replies, "*You're going to be all right. Do what needs to be done and quit worrying. Now stop with all the questions. And yes, we will always be friends.*"

Chapter 16

Living in fear of *cats* like a common field mouse was not Roedee's way of making the best out of his situation. He had special powers but he didn't like the idea that his powers had no affect on ordinary cats. He soon realizes he has to look out for himself, regardless of his friendship with Midnight, so he vanishes and reappears in the alley where Ghost Kitty and his gang are waiting.

"*I knew you'd come back*," he laughed as he ordered his gang to stand their ground between him and Roedee.

"*I'm not here to assassinate you cat. I'm here to make a deal.*" muttered the little mouse with the squeaky voice that tremors with fear.

"Yes, I'm listening."

"You promise to protect me from all the cats in the world and in exchange I promise to not terminate you. So, what do you say? Do we have a deal?"

"Sure, but what about Midnight and why haven't you asked him to protect you?" "That's my business and I don't owe you any explanation. Do we or don't we have a deal cat?"

Ghost Kitty looked at his gang and said, *"We have a deal but you have to go through the initiation if you want to join my gang, and I'm telling you right now it won't be easy. Are you up to it little mouse?"*

Roedee was desperate to find his place in the world. He felt like he could handle just about anything, but could he?

"Just name it and consider it done," boasted the little mouse.

"You must destroy Midnight, just as you have planned to destroy me," growled the ferocious white cat.

This request made Roedee very uneasy but thinking quickly he responded, *"But, I can't destroy Midnight like I can you and I wouldn't anyway because he's my friend."*

The look on Ghost Kitty's face was not a pretty sight. Roedee feared the *cats* would attack him so he vanished and reappeared next to his feline adversary. *"I won't destroy Midnight because I can't, but I will promise to keep him away from you. A deal is a deal."* Roedee wasn't being completely honest. He knew his powers could destroy Midnight but he convinced the evil cat that the only one he should fear was him.

Ghost Kitty felt powerful again. He defeated his only

known enemy, the scruffy little mouse, who not only succumbed to his greatness, but betrayed his only true friend.

As time passed Roedee had gotten to comfortable around the *cats*, so much that he started to feel invincible, that was his first mistake. He really felt like part of the gang, not just an honorary member. He truly thought he had finally found his place in the world. That was his second mistake. The evil cat and the disheveled little mouse became inseparable. Where Ghost Kitty went Roedee followed. The cat was getting annoyed.

With a swift jerk of his paw he extracted his claws and swatted the little mouse, not striking him, just giving him a warning. Roedee's reflexes were quick as the collar around his neck started to glow. The gang of hungry felines stood silent in the dimly lit alley and observed. Within minutes Ghost Kitty collapses as the members of his gang watch.

Roedee turns to them and relays a telepathic message, "*I will do to you what I did to him if you defy me.*" Taking several steps backwards, they begin to wine, "Meow, meow." They were like lost little souls and Roedee loved feeling so mighty.

Out of the darkness Midnight appears with his eyes fixed on Roedee. He can see Ghost Kitty is down and at first thinks Roedee has finally destroyed him, but his keen senses tell him he has been betrayed. The disappointment on his face is heart wrenching as he was overcome with sadness. Distraught, he could not speak.

The emotions exchanged between them at just a glance, will be forever imbedded in Roedee's mind. Its then, Roedee realizes he has lost his only true friend.

Suddenly, the gang of cats surrounds Midnight as Roedee stands between them on his back legs. His collar glows and the cats back off . Hoping Midnight appreciated his bravery, he turns to look for his disheartened friend, but he wasn't there, he vanished.

Hours passed before Ghost Kitty was able to move and after regaining his strength he realized his greatness was once again being challenged. Things had certainly changed and there wasn't anything he could do about it except surrender to the little mouse, who had now become, leader of the pack. Roedee felt a freedom like never before and he envied no one. But, his heart was heavy with sorrow and guilt. He had lost his only true friend.

As time went on, Ghost Kitty was ready to get back in charge and put Roedee where he belonged. Imagine a mouse being the leader of a gang of *Cats*. It was downright disgraceful. He had to be discreet. He would convince the little mouse to join him in his quest to destroy all humanoids by combining their powers. They would destroy anyone or anything that stood in their way. They would become leaders of the universe, but little did they know that by mingling their powers they would bring about a force so strong and so devastating that it would change their lives forever.

The chase continues, leaping from one dimension to the other. Since domestic cats were everywhere, Roedee still felt he needed protection. The dual practiced merging their powers, realizing the combination placed them in a position of superiority. Their greatest discovery was their ability to control the weather, for brief periods. But, soon they learn first hand about the wrath of Mother Nature.

"*Roedee,*" said Ghost Kitty. "*Just imagine what we can do as a team. Since we can control the weather, we can rule the world and all the humanoids will beg for their miserable lives just like I had to beg for mine when I was just a kitten.*" Roedee wasn't so sure about ruling the world if it meant harming the innocents.

"*I don't know,*" he replied. Knowing the weakness of the little mouse the cat proclaims, "*Roedee, you would finally find your place in the world. A place you have searched for all your life.*" Taking a moment to reflect he realizes this was exactly what he's always wanted. So, he agreed to help Ghost Kitty.

Their quest takes them to Oklahoma City, to the center of tornado alley, where a storm is already brewing on the horizon. Sounds of thunder shake the earth and the distant cumulus clouds are the perfect recipe to help Mother Nature generate the world's greatest and most devastating twister. Concentrating their powers on the intense thunderstorm, results in an awesome lightning display that covers the darkened sky.

Then a spectacular explosion of the super cell thunderstorm erupts into large hail and a massive wall of clouds. Their focus grows stronger as the super cell intensifies. Ghost Kitty and Roedee watch as the powerful winds of the enormous storm devour them tossing them in the center. Suddenly, a violent rotating column of air plummets to the ground and an F3 tornado is born, touching down briefly, rising back up and touching down again.

The winds inside escalated to swirls close to three hundred miles per hour expanding the vortex until it becomes four miles long and four hundred yards wide. The fury of the storm continues to grow, creating a mass of destruction and nothing in its path is spared. A swath over a mile wide travels through Oklahoma City and it suburbs, chewing up homes and demolishing everything in its path. The storm is so severe, it reaches a height of sixty thousand feet and exceeds the F5 Fujita scale and then, it simply vanished. This was the worst disaster of the millennia. The number of lives lost was greater than any other natural disaster ever recorded. But this wasn't a natural phenomenon.

After having been on the trail of Roedee and Ghost Kitty, Midnight appeared following the destruction. He couldn't believe the misery and despair caused by these wretched misfits leaving a once populated land barren and bleak. The sensitive whiskers around his mouth worked like radar and he began detecting ectoplasmic activity. His erect pointed ears acted like a directional antenna and his rounded head and short muzzle acted like a receiver.

His claws were removed from their protective sheaths as he received pulses of electromagnetic waves. As he stood there, each of the five toes on his forefeet began to pulsate. His tail waived back and forth, up and down and left to right. His search ended when he discovered Roedee under a pile of rubble. The little mouse was seriously hurt and unable to heal himself. Midnight levitates the debris off the injured mouse and places his paws on his chest. The collar around his neck glows and Roedee is healed.

Midnight lies down to rest. Roedee is so excited to see

him. He jumps up and shouts, *"You saved me and I have missed you so much."* But, as he raises his head he's surrounded by the destruction he caused, he knew he was responsible. He lowered his pointed snout in shame. He never knew a pain could voyage so deep and hurt so bad, knowing he had harmed the innocents. Roedee went to Midnight's side and begged for forgiveness but there was no response.

Ghost Kitty appeared. His powers were stronger than ever and he felt indestructible. The collar around his neck started to glow as he focused on the black motionless cat. Roedee's collar began to glow as he focused on Ghost Kitty, threatening to kill him if he didn't stop. Midnight regained his strength and focused on Ghost Kitty as the collar around his neck started to glow.

The powers exchanged between them created a rapid release of energy, producing large amounts of radioactivity. With their powers joined gamma rays generated a thermonuclear reaction forming an emission of very high energy photons and once connected they traveled faster than the speed of light. Then an amazing phenomenon occurred. Their particles collided and they took a quantum leap and traveled back in time before the disastrous storm. They ended up right back where they started, in tornado alley prior to the massive destruction.

They heard a low pulsating hum followed by a piercing screech and a high pitched ring, and that all too familiar smell, sulfur. Lights flashed in a rotating motion. First red and then green, and finally blue, and out of the blue light came a brilliant white light, which burst into the radiant twinkle of a distant star.

Roedee was first to awaken as he shook the dust off his hairless tail. Inspecting his paws he noticed his pads were black. Ghost Kitty noticed his pads were black and Midnight's pads were white. They gathered in a circle and gazed at the distant star which spoke to them.

"*You are now brothers, destined to protect the innocents. You are 'Ghost Riders In The Sky.' You will be seen as red eyed, fire-breathing, superheroes; a band of heavenly riders who storm across the endless sky advocating goodness. You will proclaim to mankind to either change their evil ways or be caught by the devil and doomed forever. You are now immortal beings ordained to fight wickedness and free the world from destruction and save the righteous.*"

"*What's going on?*" asked the little mouse. Ghost Kitty with haste jumped up and took that all too familiar stance, ready to fight, but, he felt very odd.

"*Hey,*" he said.

"*What's going on? I feel funny.*" Midnight was just as confused.

"*What happened to us?*" asked Roedee.

Ghost Kitty sighed, looked at Midnight and says, "*I don't want to harm the humanoids any more. Everything you said was true. Not all humanoids are evil. I should have listened to you. I have hurt so many people.*"

For the very first time since chasing his mutant clone, Midnight felt relief knowing the battle was over. He raised his head and looked at his two brothers and said, "*Look around. The devastation you caused never happened. Somehow, when our powers merged, we turned back time and became joined as one. My desire to return home is gone because I am home and the two of you are my family.*"

They touched noses sealing an eternal bond and then off they went hopping from one dimension to the other. The chase was still on but this time it was with a commitment to each other to help those in need.

Chapter 17

It had been sometime since the trio had been to the lab and when they returned, their visit wasn't totally welcomed. But, Thomas was delighted to see his little buddy. "Midnight, how are you? I have really missed you little guy. Telesa will be so happy to see you," he said as he hugged his furry feline friend. Looking over his shoulder he observed his two companions.

"Is that Ghost Kitty and Roedee? They seem different. In fact, you all seem different."

Purring loudly Midnight was very pleased to see his favorite humanoid and said, "*We are different, very different.*" The professor entered the room, stopped and stared in horror as she relived the memories of their recent past. The trio set their collars aglow and her fears were put to rest.

"*Marian,*" said Midnight. "*We are no longer enemies. We have been joined together as one to protect the innocents. We are animals with human intelligence with superpowers. A distant star granted us immortality and our destiny has been chosen to serve mankind. We are more powerful than ever before, each equal in the powers we possess, united to fight evil and we are all a part of the professor.*"

She understood completely. Over the recent months she came to the same conclusion that the trio and the professor were somehow connected. *Could it be that the professor used some of his own DNA when he saved Midnight? And could it be that part of the professor was passed onto Ghost Kitty and Roedee through Midnight?* She tried to conceive such an outlandish theory.

Ghost Kitty stepped forward facing both the professor and Thomas. He looked grand with his long white fur and soft flawless mane around his huge round head. He said with all sincerity, "*I'm sorry for the harm I caused you. Will you please forgive me?*"

Lowering his head in disgrace, both the professor and Thomas commenced petting him, giving him the reassurance he needed, knowing he had been forgiven. Roedee interrupted, when he too apologized. "*Professor,*" he mumbled. "*I'm sorry I didn't do what I was supposed to and destroy that evil cat, but I did try, and all I've got to show for it is this fluffy white coat. And even worse, did you know that cats can eat me?*"

Taking Roedee in the palm of her hand, she kissed him

on the tip of his nose and said, "You're a good boy Roedee and I'm very proud of you." His little face lit up like a candle. For the very first time in his existence he came to know the true meaning of unconditional love. At that moment, a beautiful silver pendant, appeared on his collar and revealed his name *Roedee*. He had finally found his place in the world.

Over the course of the next few days the trio tested the extent of their powers and discovered immortality wasn't so bad, they were invincible and nothing could ever harm them. "Thomas," said the professor. "I need to talk to you about a recent development in connection with the professor's DNA. Somehow he seems to be one of the key sources to our magical little friends, which I still have a problem believing really exist. If I hadn't experienced them first hand I would have never believed it possible, and a part of me still doesn't, because of the lack of scientific evidence."

Thomas smiled and said, "I understand professor. What do you want me to do?" She opened her laptop and showed him the genome mapping she prepared using the DNA of Professor ReMax salvaged from the fire. He glanced at the variance table and reviewed the chromosomal DNA sequencing and cloning strategy and was startled by what he saw. He asked, "Is this possible professor? Can you really clone the professor?"

She stood next to the decompression chamber and slightly emotional she proclaimed, "I can. However, my theory is incomplete. I will need to extract DNA from each of our superheroes and add it to the human genome and reconstruct the way the genes are written in the human chromosomes."

Thomas stared at Marian and asked, "But, how can you cross match their DNA? Everyone knows you can't cross animal DNA with humans. It's never been done."

She responded, "Yes, we can with the decompression chamber, we just need a segment of the DNA called exons. We can transcribe the exons into RNA and translate them into protein. The exons are fused into a continuous message and when the gene is activated, the result is a mutation. Don't you see that's how Midnight was cloned."

"The combination of chemicals, the professor's DNA, and the radioactive response from the decompression chamber produced the mutation."

"But, you know the problems the professor had with his experiment. The clone lived in a vegetative state."

"Yes, because he didn't use the correct formula. Remember we found that missing link with Ghost Kitty."

"Yeah, and he turned out evil. What are you planning to do to keep that from happening again?"

"That's why I need the DNA from each of the trio. It will restore balance between good and evil. It will work Thomas. I know it will work and it will bring back the professor."

Quietly, they mulled over the idea of seeing the professor again. But, several factors had to be explored other than the mere possibility. Thomas looked at her and asked, "Marian, what about Jonathan? Are you going to tell him? How do you think he's going to feel about you bringing his father back from the dead?" She took a deep breath and exhaled slowly.

"It's science Thomas. It's what his father would have wanted. It's what he worked his entire life to achieve. Why shouldn't he be the one to benefit from his years of research?"

He asked again, "Are you going to tell Jonathan?"

With a subdued look she responded with a definite, "No."

The following day, in preparation of the experiment, the trio's DNA was collected using their salvia, blood, hair strands, skin samples, and claws.

It was soon time for the trio to depart but not until after Midnight got to see his second most favorite humanoid, Telesa. He followed Thomas out of the lab and into their quarters and as the door to the kitchen opened, there stood Telesa as beautiful as he remembered.

"Oh, for heavens sake," she cried. "It's Midnight. When did you get back? I have missed you so much," She picked him up and cuddled him in her arms.

"I've missed you too, Telesa but my visit will be short. We have much work to do," he purred.

"We?" she asked.

"Yes, along with Ghost Kitty and Roedee," whom she knew nothing about.

"Oh," she said, "You've picked up some friends along the way have you?"

He didn't try to explain. Then much to his surprise she blurted, "You're Ghost Riders and your mission will be to protect the innocents." Thomas stared at Midnight with an exacerbated look when she said, "Yes, ever since I was healed that night, I've been able to sense things. Not all things mind you, just certain things that have a connection to me. Like you, Midnight. I know everything you've been through these past few months even though I wasn't there, but I somehow know. It sounds crazy and I don't understand it myself."

Thomas asked, "Why haven't you said something, honey? You've been able to sense things about me ever since that night in Chiptaw?" With the sweet tenderness of her smile she nodded her head, leaving her husband totally dumbfounded.

Returning to the lab, Thomas had to share the professor's plan with Midnight. "Little buddy, I need to tell you something about the work we're doing," the words stumbled out of his mouth.

"It's okay Thomas. I know what Marian is planning. I knew, before she knew and it's the right thing to do. Just remember, I will always be here to protect you." Their goodbyes were said and Midnight and his Ghost Riders departed.

Their next destination was the skyscraper in Manhattan where they made a visit to Jonathan's law office. As Jonathan opened the door, he observed two cats and a mouse sitting on top of his papers sprawled across his desk. At least those they didn't knock onto the floor. "Some things never change do they Midnight?" he laughed as he sat in his chair and reclined backwards. "So, who are your friends?"

Jonathan recognized Ghost Kitty. At that moment the cat spoke, *"I'm sorry for the harm I caused you. Will you please forgive me?"* He lowered his head in shame. The collar around his neck started to glow and Jonathan realized he was safe.

Reaching his hand forward, he placed it gently on the head of the now humble cat and said, "I do forgive you Ghost Kitty. I do forgive you." And their mission was accomplished; they vanished.

Their journey took them to the small town of Chiptaw to see Papa and Mama. "Hey-a Mama," said Papa. "It's-a Midnight, and he brought-a his friends. Come in Midnight, and bring-a you friends." As the trio entered the kitchen, Mama stood frozen in her steps, she was unable to speak. "Mama," said Papa. "What's-a wrong with you? It's-a Midnight and his little friends."

Ghost Kitty took a stately pose when they heard him utter the words, *"I'm sorry for the harm I caused you. Will you please forgive me?"* They were mortified but curious. A cat who could talk? Not just a cat, but the cat who tried to drown them. The collar around his neck started to glow as Midnight and Roedee joined in, and Papa and Mama knew they had nothing to fear.

"Papa," said Mama. "He's-a good boy and he didn't-a mean to hurt us. What-a you say we forgive and forget?" Papa shook his head in agreement and patted each of the trio on the top of their heads as the trio faded away.

Next they trekked to the hub of Boston, Massachusetts where Paul Revere, on his famous ride along the brick layered streets, yelled, "The British are coming! The British are coming!" Amanda Renee and her mother Tasha Marie were having lunch at a quaint but luxurious café, which lined the red brick street where the cheapest thing on the menu was a $20 croissant surrounded by strawberries and a fancy green garnish.

The trio appeared outside the railing next to the bistro table where they sat, and Roedee was not an accepted guest. Tasha Marie was truly insulted that such a fine establishment would allow *mice*. As the waiter approached she of course complained.

"I will never, ever return to this eatery because you have *mice*."

The waiter looked around and saw nothing and boasted, "Madam, I assure you we do not have mice." Amanda Renee started to laugh, because she could see the little mouse sitting between the two cats.

"I'm telling you there is a mouse and two cats outside this railing staring at us, and I want them removed immediately," she yelled. Her anger turned to fear as she became aware of the presence of Ghost Kitty.

The trio's collars illuminated, calming her fears when she heard the noble cat say, *"I'm sorry for the harm I caused you. Will you please forgive me?"*

For the first time in her entire life Tasha Marie was speechless. Amanda Renee kept laughing and said, "Mother, it's the cat from the boat before I fell off, and he can talk. Cool. Can we keep him?" She still had nothing to say. She took her coat and her daughter, and left.

Midnight looked at Ghost Kitty and meowed as he nudged him with the top of his head and said, *"You tried your best and we're proud of you. Just remember, not all humanoids are forgiving, especially those who can't forgive themselves.*" Roedee climbed on the back of Ghost Kitty and the trio was off.

Chapter 18

Meanwhile, back at the lab, Marian and Thomas completed the final preparations to clone Professor ReMax using both his DNA and segments of DNA from the three superheroes. It was a very tedious process and the chemical combination had to be exact. One mistake and the entire experiment could fail or worse, bring back an evil genetic mutation.

"Thomas, now that we have the professor's DNA, I have taken the nucleus from one of the cells and have organized its structure into chromosomes to make up the genome. With DNA replication I have duplicated the chromosomes for future use, in the event we have a problem. I've added some DNA from each of the animals and after the cells completely divide we'll be ready to introduce the DNA embryo into a suitable host. I am using bacterial plasmids to generate multiple copies of the gene and once the transformation takes place, we'll use the stem cells as a repair kit. After the embryo is placed in the decompression chamber and exposed to the cycle of lights, we should have our clone. Are you ready?" she asked.

With the nod of his head they proceeded with the experiment, placing the embryo in the decompression chamber and triggering switches two, three, and nine. The rotation of lights went exactly as planned. First a flash of red, green, and blue; out of the blue light there came a brilliant white light, followed by a low pulsating hum, a piercing screech and a high pitched ring. And as expected, the entire process stopped. The room grew quiet and the lights went dim as the odor of the chemicals diminished.

Thomas stood quietly by the chamber, hesitating to open the door. Marian said, "Go ahead, it's now or never." As the door opened, he looked inside and saw nothing but a dark chamber. The steel walls were coated with black-looking soot. "Professor, you've got to see this ... it looks like we blew up the embryo or something." When she looked inside she felt something move past her. She caught a glance of a shadow at the edge of her field of vision, for just a split second.

"Thomas, did you see that? Did you see the dark form of a figure?"

"No, I didn't see anything," he said. After only seconds the shadows reappeared and this time they both saw two shapeless masses, forming and disintegrating. They were black humanoid silhouettes with no discernable mouths or noses, and they had glowing red eyes. "Professor, what are these things?"

They moved slowly and then rapidly and when they came into view they hopped from one part of the room to the other where they lingered and then vanished. "Professor, what's going on?" Searching for some scientific rationale she finally said, "It must be a collection of negative psychic energy or another dimensional being whose dimension or origin has overlapped ours. Somehow, they've gained access to our world through the decompression chamber."

Thomas asked, "You mean, they're aliens?"

"I mean they're some sort of supernatural phenomenon that I can't explain, just like I can't explain our little superheroes."

Talking out loud, Marian tried to find the logic in the situation. "Are they paranormal apparitions? Have we been working so hard, that our imagination is playing tricks on us? You know Thomas, the human mind and eye can be fooled very easily. I think these dark shadowy figures are just illusions."

However, the illusions continued to appear. They had a distinct human shape and as soon as they showed themselves, their form fell apart leaving behind an unusual yet familiar odor, the same odor they recreated in the lab. The professor finally declared, "We have been invaded by interdemensional beings, time travelers, if you will. Something seen but they have no physical reality, no bodies. They are only shadows, but they seem to feed off our energy."

Unbeknownst to the Professor, they were the ultimate essence of pure evil, with their glowing red eyes that entered our dimension for a purpose, and one purpose only. "But what happened to Professor ReMax?" she asked. "My calculations were precise. Could this be a mutated form of the professor?" Then as quickly as they came, they went, leaving behind small traces of gamma radiation.

Inspecting the chamber Marian noticed the steel walls were once again bright and shiny. "Thomas, we must take another embryo and try again. I know this experiment will work. We can't give up now, we're too close, I can feel it," she proclaimed. So, with great expectations, they placed another embryo in the chamber and triggered switches two, three, and nine. Each step was followed with exact precision until the sequence was completed.

She opened the large metal door and inside she saw the form of a man lying naked on the floor, alive and breathing. "Thomas, come and look. Help me get him on the gurney." They placed the man on the gurney and rolled him out of the chamber. Thomas covered him with a sheet while Marian took his vitals.

"The same as before, a breathing, living being but no heartbeat," she said. The man looked to be a younger version of the professor, but they couldn't be certain. Thomas declared, "What do you know, a fully formed human being who came from a tiny embryo created through a series of lights in a decompression chamber.

Who knew? This is incredible professor, but, will he stay in this vegetative state?"

"Not if I have anything to say about it," she moaned, as she injected the clone with its first dose of chemicals. "Now, all we can do is wait and see." And they waited until it was time to inject the clone with a second dose and then a third. Time passed slowly, but she wouldn't give up. "He's alive Thomas, but what did I miss? I was sure I corrected the deficiency. This shouldn't have happened."

The trio appeared with their collars aglow, as each of them circled the clone. "Midnight, what's going on?" asked Marian.

"Professor, he needs our life force. You have done all you can. The rest is up to us."

Roedee sniffed the air and wiggled his tail, having it act as a receiver, as Ghost Kitty started kneading the crown of the clone's head. Midnight climbed on the chest of the clone, placed his mouth over its mouth, and inhaled deeply, pulling all the oxygen out of the lungs. With one gigantic breath, Midnight exhaled breathing life into the listless body. The clone jerked and moved and as his eyes opened, he tried hard to focus. He tried to speak but he couldn't, he was too weak.

Immediately, the room filled again with the shadow entities that hovered over the table. Ghost Kitty reacted, hissing and growling, as his eyes turned fire red. And the ominous black shadows faded away, as quickly as they came.

All eyes were upon the man on the gurney who spoke his first words. "Midnight, it's nice to see you again. Where am I and how did I get here?"

"You must rest professor. We have much work to do, but first you must rest."

Thomas grew faint as he realized the professor had actually returned from the dead. "Marian, can this really be happening? Is this really the professor?"

She was so overcome she had to sit down and gather her thoughts. Midnight came to her and said, *"Marian, it is the professor. With giving him our life force he will remember everything about his past. The genetic mutations you engineered have brought him back healthier and stronger than before."*

She asked, "But why doesn't he have a heartbeat when he's supposed to be human?" The forlorn cat said, *"Because he's a mutant and he has no soul."*

She remembered the intruders and told Midnight, "The shadows, they escaped from the decompression chamber. Do you know why they're here? Somehow the chamber acted like a doorway from a different plane of existence, and they came through. They are very evil. Some sort of phantasm, I suspect."

"Yes, I know. They are the reason why it was vital you succeed in bringing back the professor. He is the key to their demise. Everything that has happened here today is part of your destiny." Midnight curled up next to her and as she stroked his fur the collar around his neck glowed and she felt at peace.

As the evening passed, the trio stood guard over the professor in case the shadow entities returned. Midnight and Ghost Kitty had a long cat to cat talk; they soon discovered that the shadow people were the humanoids they remembered from kitten hood. They were exposed to experiments, tortured and drained of their energy, and then tossed aside like they were nothing.

For the very first time Ghost Kitty understood the struggle with his past, as the mystery of his haunted memories unfold. His goal now was to even the score, while protecting the innocents. Roedee lay quietly next to the professor, not understanding his full connection with this humanoid, but nonetheless, he was very happy and content.

The next morning, Marian, Thomas, and the trio were there when the professor awoke. He looked to be in his mid fifties, a younger, much more handsome version of himself. He seemed a little taller and physically fit. His dark hair was graying slightly at the temples and at this age he looked remarkably like his son. But Marian knew Jonathan could never know, because he would never forgive her.

"Professor, I don't know what to say. I'm Marian Rutherford and I followed your recipe making just a few adjustments and well here you are, alive and well. I can't explain it, but I do know your existence has something to do with that decompression chamber you invented."

Thomas stepped forward and shook the professor's hand. "Is it really you, sir?"

"Yes, my boy, it's me, but I must say I feel very odd. I'm breathing and my organs seem to be functioning, but something is missing. Professor Rutherford, can you enlighten me with your perception?"

With an anxious look she glared at the regal black cat and asked, "Why don't you explain it to him Midnight?"

His furry old friend sat across from him and disclosed, *"You are a mutation of yourself, just like me, and we have no beating hearts because we have no souls. The blood that flows through our veins has been chemically induced to mimic life. We feel human emotions but we are immortal. Our immortality exists, because we are part of one another. Do you understand?"*

The professor thought he had awakened from a bad dream, when in reality he had returned from the dead. Looking at his reflection in the mirror, he saw the image of a man he barely recognized and gasped, "So, the cloning has been a success and you say we are immortal? This is marvelous. Look at me, I'm some thirty years younger, yet, I remember everything up until my death. Professor Rutherford, we must get to work and determine exactly how this happened."

Thomas chuckled and said, "First, we better get you some clothes. We can't have you walking around like that, sir."

Embarrassed, he replied, "Yes, of course my boy, you're absolutely right. I'll just call my tailor. Say, where are we exactly?"

Marian explained, "Professor, no one can know of your existence, especially your son. We're in Long Island and with the funds you left, Jonathan built this lab, but he must never know what we have done. He will never forgive me for bringing you back." The professor roared, "That's nonsense Marian. Of course he'll understand, he's my son." He was the same old professor, as head strong as ever, and he wasn't going to be reasoned with on this subject.

Chapter 19

Meanwhile, Mallory Malone was in Chiptaw trying to locate Spencer, as she suspected he had run off with her part of the money from the sting, and she wasn't about to let him get away. She asked around town and noticed people were pretty hush, hush about the man. However, before leaving she stopped in at Papa and Mama's for a bite to eat. She entered the restaurant with her long blonde hair flowing softly across her shoulders. Papa instantly noticed the attractive woman, with the slim figure.

"Welcome to Papa and Mama's. This-a way please. I gotta perfect table for you." As he helped her to her chair she said a gracious thank you as she was seated. "We gotta the best food in town," he gloated. "You choose-a any dish and I'll prepare it especially for you." She studied the menu and selected the Fettuccini Alfredo. "Oh, that's a good choice. It was the professor's favorite."

"Are you speaking of Professor ReMax?" she asked.

"Oh, yes. You know-a him, no?"

"No, we've never met but I'm in town to see him, but. . . . " She was interrupted by Papa. "Oh, no, you can't-a see him, he's a dead. Poor man, he's a dead." Mama came from the kitchen and heard Papa talking to the young woman.

"Hey-a Mama, this girl, she's-a looking for the professor."

Mama looked the woman up and down and asked, "Why-a you lookin' for the professor?"

She smiled and extended her hand and said, "Hello, I'm Mallory Malone and I represent the chemical company where the professor purchases his supplies. Since we haven't had an order from him for some time, the company sent me, to find out why. I see why now and it saddens me to hear of his passing." Mama's suspicions were put at ease as they shared their story about the professor.

Before Mallory left that evening, she learned that the faithful lab assistant was now working in Long Island and that Spencer had disappeared without a trace, and without the money. Was this the end of the sting of a lifetime? She thought not, knowing that Thomas and his millionaire bride would be her next mark. Little did she know just how much her future was about to unfold.

It was springtime in New York and the Hamptons were exceptionally beautiful this time of year. Cool, gentle breezes crossed the ocean, spraying the shore with salt water and fine granules of white sand. Seagulls glided over the shallow waves searching for their next meal. Birds of all shapes and sizes followed close behind, nibbling on left over morsels of food. Sea turtles came ashore in the black of night to lay their eggs and cover them with sand, only to leave their young to fend for themselves and return to the sea.

Mother Nature was at peace with the world, but something horrific was brewing in the lab. The professor learned more about his clone, as he pieced together the sequence of events that returned him to his mutated state. He was troubled. How could he feel emotions like love, hate, and sorrow and yet, not possess a soul? But one thing he still had, and stronger than ever, was an extraordinary compassion for mankind. His quest to produce the perfect genetic specimen was not a priority. The purpose of his mere existence was to save mankind. *But how?*

The trio appeared. "*It's time to begin our work professor,*" said Midnight.

"*Me too,*" said Roedee. "*I want to help.*"

"*Yeah, well I'm ready to rid the world of those Shadow People,*" boasted Ghost Kitty.

"Calm down, all of you," said the professor.

"There's still much to do before the battle."

Marian entered the lab with another injection she prepared. It seemed the professor needed to be injected every couple of days in order to maintain balance in his chemically induced blood. If he missed an injection, he would become very weak and return to a vegetative state.

Sitting next to the professor Midnight explained. "*You must find a way to stop using the chemicals; they are preventing you from utilizing your powers.*"

"But, if he doesn't have the injections he'll return to being a zombie," stated Marian. "*There has to be another way,*" said Midnight. "*You must keep searching.*"

The lab was infiltrated with dark shadows, this time, they filled the room. With their fiery red eyes, they surrounded the trio. They would hold their form, disintegrate and reform. They continued this cycle over and over until the trio's collars lit up and the cowardly beings fled.

"*Now that's what I'm talkin' about,*" shouted Roedee as he stood up on his hind legs and wiggled his nose.

"*Yeah, you miserable.... That'll teach you,*" bragged Ghost Kitty.

With diligence, they spent hours looking over the notes of the recent experiment that brought back the professor. They went from beginning to end, hoping to find some clue as to the reason for the vegetative state, but nothing was discovered.

Marian came to the conclusion that the difference between the human clone and the animals was the mixture of DNA. Perhaps she used too little of the animal DNA in the professor, because the trio didn't need any injections.

"Marian, tell me about the stem cells you preserved to use as a repair kit," asked the professor.

"Well, I used bacterial plasmids to generate multiple copies of the gene, and once the transformation took place we had a supply of stem cells. But sir, could it be that simple?" she asked.

The professor rubbed his chin as he sat mulling it over. "Now, let's just think about this for a minute, my dear. We know that stem cells have the ability to develop into many different types of cells, serving as a sort of repair system for the body. They can divide without limit to replenish other cells. If we can find a way to train the stem cells to divide, and become red blood cells, then that just may solve the problem and I can quit getting all these injections. What do you think Marian?"

Bewildered, she said, "Sir, your theory is impossible. How in the world can we train stem cells?"

"Oh, we'll find a way, my dear, we'll find a way."

Midnight sitting quietly listened to the debate between the two great scientific minds and asked, *"Why can't you inject the stem cells with the chemicals and let them reproduce?"*

The professor laughed, "Midnight, you're smarter than the average house cat. Don't you see Marian? If we inject the genetically altered stem cells and place them with human red blood cells, then they'll continue to divide and renew themselves until we have enough to switch out the chemically induced blood with the red blood cells." Marian rolled back her eyes in disbelief and said, "But, you have no heart to pump the blood."

"So, I'll build a heart, let's get started."

When Mallory Malone stepped off the plane at JFK Airport in New York, she arranged for a limo to take her to Long Island, where she rented a room at an exquisite hotel in the Hamptons. Her goal was to contact Thomas Sheffield and con him out of a nice chunk of his millions. Since he was now married and had a million dollar bride, the ideal plan was blackmail. But, she had problems locating the lab. After a thorough search of the entire island she was infuriated. There weren't many challenges this seasoned con woman couldn't handle but to be defeated before she even got started wasn't an option.

She took a walk along the sandy beach on the east side and came upon a most unusual building whose design didn't fit the landscape. Closer inspection she noted a state of the art security system and realized this was the lab. *Um ... How obvious she thought.*

She watched the comings and goings over the next few days of anyone and everyone who entered and left the building. Finally she located her mark, and followed Thomas and Telesa into Manhattan, where they met Jonathan and Marian for dinner. She didn't have a reservation, but that didn't stop her. She managed to get a table nearby and using a crafty listening device, she could hear everything being said.

"It's nice that everyone came to town for dinner, but it would have been a lot easier if I'd of met you at the lab," said Jonathan.

"Oh, no," said Marian. "I was looking forward to coming into the city and seeing you. It's hard being there day after day." He smiled and took her hand. The dinner conversation was superficial and dry, like they were both hiding some big secret. Telesa knew Thomas was covering up something. She wanted to know exactly what it was and she had every intention of finding out.

Meanwhile, back at the lab, the professor and the trio were discussing the *Shadow People* when Roedee asked, *"Where do these shadow things come from professor?"*

He raised his eyebrows and tried to reassure the little mouse and said, "They come from '*Somewhere Over The Rainbow*' way up high and you needn't be afraid. We will be able to conquer them once we know why they're here."

"But, why are they here professor?" asked Ghost Kitty. *"And why did they torture us when we were just kittens?"*

The professor surmised, "Well, my educated guess is that our planet has something they need, perhaps to save their own species. I know they are drawn to this lab, so that something must be here. We need to figure out what that is, and decide if we want to give it to them."

Midnight asked, *"But, why would we want to give them anything? They are pure evil; they mean to destroy the human race."*

The party of four finished their dinner and Marian spent the night in the city. During the drive home from Manhattan to the Hamptons, the car was quiet. It was obvious, thought Telesa, that Thomas was hiding something, but she couldn't zone in on what, not even with her newly found sixth sense.

In that instant the car in front stopped suddenly and Thomas slammed on the brakes, just missing the vehicle ahead by a few inches. The car sped away and within seconds the car behind ploughed into the rear of the

Mustang. It was Mallory Malone and she took advantage of this unexpected mishap.

As they got out of their cars and stood on the side of the road Mallory asked, "Is everyone all right?" Thomas couldn't help but notice the attractive blonde.

"Yes, we're fine," said Thomas.

"Well, if I live and breathe, Thomas Sheffield," said the nice looking woman.

"I haven't seen you in years. How have you been?" Of course, he had no clue who she was but he wasn't quite sure. They exchanged driver information and decided to not call the police.

"I'm so sorry. I'll be glad to take care of the damages," she insisted. "That's the least I can do for that once special man in my life."

By now Thomas was really confused. So was Telesa, who blatantly introduced herself. "I'm Telesa Sheffield, Thomas' wife." The look between them was merciless. The seed had been planted and they depart.

"Who was that woman Thomas?" demanded Telesa.

"Honey, I have no idea. I can't remember her at all."

"Well, you acted like you knew her."

"I just didn't want to be rude."

Yes, the lonely lab assistant slept on the couch that night, trying his best to remember that woman, but he had no recollection of her whatsoever.

The next morning was very awkward. Telesa wasn't speaking to Thomas, so he went to work. "Good morning professor. Marian will be in a little late. She stayed in town last night." The professor looked run down, he needed another injection. "Sir, let me help you. You're getting weaker, let me give you an injection."

"No, my boy, I must wait. The stem cells are just about finished dividing and reproducing with the red blood cells. They'll be ready shortly, for the transfusion. Come here and let me show you my latest invention. My mechanical heart." It looked and worked just like a human heart.

"You see my boy, this ventricular assist device consists of a blood tube, by which the blood will be pooled into this one area, and this pressure sensor will pump the blood through the arteries and veins, thus keeping me out of the vegetative state. And since we have injected the stem cells with the chemicals, if all goes well, I won't need anymore injections." This was way too complicated for Thomas to understand, but he trusted the professor's instincts and hoped the transfusion would work.

All preparations were made. The stem cells completed their division and reproduced into a vast supply of red blood cells. Marian proceeded to implant the device in the professor's chest and began the transfusion.

As the chemicals were drained from his body, and replaced with red blood cells, the professor would go in and out of consciousness, but he seemed to be adapting well. The mechanical heart worked as anticipated and it appeared the experiment was going to succeed, until the *Shadow People* returned, taking form over the professor.

"Thomas, quick, call the trio, we need their help." They encircled the room, with their collars glowing, but the shadowy figures maintained their form as their fiery eyes drained the life force out of the professor.

"Midnight, do, something!" begged Marian.

Much to their surprise, the professor sat up on the gurney and with his eyes closed he spoke, *"Behold, I will destroy all evil upon the face of the earth and become a living human soul. Be gone before my eyes are opened."* And hence, they vanished.

At that moment a clear, seamless bracelet appeared on his right ankle as he climbed off the gurney.

"Sir, look, you have the same mysterious collar around your ankle, and it glows just like the trio's. What does it mean?" asked Thomas.

"It means my boy that the implant of the artificial heart and transfusion was a success and I now possess the same powers as the trio; we are united as one. Thomas, I must apologize for not believing you."

"When sir?"

"When you told me Midnight used to speak to you. My boy, he was once victimized by these shadowy creatures and after exposing him to their experiments, he gained the knowledge of speech just as I have now gained the knowledge of their existence. I know why they are here, and I understand why they must be stopped."

Marian asked, "What can we do to help professor?"

Taking a comfortable seat, surrounded by the trio he explained, "They are from the planet *Mewzak* and they have come to Earth, home of the human race, for our *Kyanite Crystals*, which cover seventy five percent of the earths surface. The crystals, to us, are simply a mineral, but it has great value to the shadow entities, because when it is heated at extreme temperatures it undergoes irreversible expansion, and becomes a solid mass."

"This mass enables them to take form and walk the earth in order to conquer the human species. In their present form they can jump from being a two dimensional shadow, to a three dimensional shadow, and take quantum leaps from one dimension to the other, just like the trio. They have been here for some time, and have used my decompression chamber to gain access. The chamber must be destroyed."

Marian sighed and said, "But professor, if we destroy the chamber, we will destroy all evidence of your existence and the existence of the trio."

"Yes, my dear, but if we don't, then they will destroy mankind."

With the nod of her head she understood but questioned, "Why are they so attracted to the lab? What's here they need?"

"Chemicals, my dear, not just any chemicals, mind you, but the combination we produced. It gives them the ability to excavate the crystals. We will need the power of the eternal most high in order to conquer these creatures." At that moment they vanished.

"This is unbelievable," she said as she glared at Thomas. "Remember Marian, what the professor always taught you, to believe in the impossible?" She left and joined Jonathan in the city.

Chapter 20

After such a long day, Thomas was exhausted. A little reluctant to return home, knowing Telesa may still be very angry with him, he decided to take a walk along the seashore and watch the sunset. He sauntered along with his hands in his pockets, thinking about the day's events and his future survival now that he knew the purpose of the shadow entities. Nothing else mattered but saving mankind. But of course, who should he run into while walking along the beach but Mallory Malone.

"Hello, Thomas, fancy meeting you here. I called today to make arrangements to get your car fixed and I spoke to your wife. Did she give you the message?"

He shook his head and said, "No, I haven't been home yet." He looked tired.

"Listen, you look pretty wiped out. Why don't we go and have a drink, relax, and talk over old times." He still had no idea who this woman was or how she fit into his past, but he agreed to meet her for a drink. They took separate cars, and met just up the road at O'Malley's Bar and Grill.

Their discussion was light hearted, but Mallory did her homework. "Thomas, it's so wonderful seeing you again after all these years. I remember the last time we saw each other in Missouri. You stood there in your black suit and tie and wished me well as I left for school. I never dreamed I would ever run into you again and here we are, it must be fate."

He was still dumbfounded. He had no remembrance of this woman at all, and as he was about to admit it, who should walk in but Telesa. As she approached Thomas from behind, Mallory took advantage of the situation. She jumped in his lap and planted a big wet kiss on his mouth, leaving the outline of her big red lips on his darkly tanned skin.

Catching the kiss, Telesa rushed to the table and demanded an explanation. "Thomas, what is going on? Why are you here with that woman and why were you kissing her?"

As he stood he said, "Honey, I wasn't kissing her, she was kissing me."

"Well, that's just fine. Another woman's lipstick all over my husband's mouth." Mallory tried to intercede, "Please Mrs. Sheffield let me explain."

"There is nothing for you to explain. If you want him so badly, you can have him. I'm going back to Chiptaw."

She stormed out of the bar, got into her SUV, and left as Thomas ran after her, seeing only road dust left by her speeding car. Mallory was close behind. "I'm sorry Thomas. I didn't mean to cause a problem. I just felt overwhelmed and had to kiss you. Will you please forgive me?"

Without exchanging words, he left and headed home to try and reason with Telesa, but when he arrived she wasn't there. He feared she may have meant what she said. He tried to reach her on her cell, but she wasn't answering. He left several messages. After an hour or so he thought for sure she would have called, but still no word.

He couldn't sleep, so he went to check on the lab. When he turned on the lights he saw the shadow entities. The room was filled with their smoke colored silhouettes, and he could feel their negative energy. They were jumping from one side of the room to the other, with their eyes glowing red. The chamber door was open and there were as many going in as there were coming out. The smell of sulfur was very strong and Thomas realized they were after the chemicals. He had to stop them, but how?

He called for the professor and the trio but they didn't come. The shadows backed him up against the wall with an electromagnetic field; he could not move. He could sense their evil and he feared for his life. Without warning they left leaving behind that familiar smell. The room grew bright again, and he was released.

"Whoa, I don't want to ever go through that again." He started shouting, "Midnight, can you hear me? You have to bring back the professor," but there was no response. "I don't guess calling 911 will help."

He returned to his quarters and tried calling Telesa's cell again, but she still wouldn't answer. Finally, totally exhausted, he collapsed on the bed and fell asleep. After a few hours he heard a knock at the door.

"Thomas, are you there?" It was Professor Rutherford. "Thomas, are you there?" she shouted.

"I'm coming," he said with a groggy voice.

When he opened the door, he saw the look on her face and said, "I 'm sorry Marian. I didn't know how to stop them. I called for the professor and Midnight but they didn't come. Do you think something has happened to them?"

"Of course not, they're supposed to be immortal. Come with me, I want to show you something."

When they entered the lab, it was like a twister had been through the room. "Wow, I don't remember there being this much damage last night," he said. "My guess is there wasn't. By the looks of this place they've been back several times. Obviously they have been successful in extracting the *kyanite crystals*."

Concerned, he asked, "Exactly what does that mean Marian?"

With the raise of her eyebrows she said, "Well, according to the professor, it means they are now able to take form and walk the earth."

Thomas knew he had no control over the situation, but the way his life was going he felt like he didn't have control over anything.

"It's not your fault Thomas. There was nothing you could have done."

"Yeah, I know that's not it; Telesa left me last night to go back to Chiptaw."

"Well, whatever for?"

"It's a long story. Let's clean up this mess and get back to work. I need to keep busy."

As they started getting the lab organized, they had an unexpected visitor. "Good morning and what a beautiful morning it is, I must say."

Seeing the lab in such disarray Jonathan asked, "Hey, what the heck happened? Is everyone alright? Did you have a break-in? What happened to the security system?"

Marian tried to calm him down. "Jonathan, we're fine. What brings you here so early this morning?"

"You, my darling. I couldn't start my day without seeing you," he said as they embraced. "Well, what a nice surprise. Will you be staying long?" He sensed she didn't want him around. "Don't you want me to stay?"

"Well, of course, it's just that we have so much to do, and the lab is in such a mess."

"Then I will take the day off and help you clean up."

"Oh, no, you needn't do that, dear."

"Of course I do, I want to spend the day with you. Now tell me what can I do?" She could see it was useless to try and send him away, but she should have tried harder, because who should appear but the professor and the trio, and they materialized right in front of their unsuspecting guest.

"Jonathan, my son, so nice to see you," gleamed the professor.

"Dad, is that really you? But, how in the world did you ... Marian ... what's going on here and what have you done?" he shouted.

"Son, she didn't do anything I wouldn't have done. You mustn't be angry with her. You have to understand, we're scientists, and what we have accomplished is critical to the future survival of this planet."

Marian sat quietly while the professor tried to reason with his son. "Jonathan, I am the result of all my years of labor and Marian has made it possible for me to live again, through a cloned body. Yes, it has some flaws but we think we've corrected the problems. There are more important matters at hand we need to discuss, other than my returning from the dead."

Jonathan studied the face of his father, the build of his physique and said, "My goodness, it really is you, Dad. You look about my age. I remember when you were in your fifties and you still look the same. This is incredible," he said as he drew his father to his chest and embraced him tightly.

"I knew you'd come around my boy."

Marian, still afraid to speak uttered the words, "I'm sorry to put you through this but ..." Jonathan took her in his arms and said, "But, you have and it's a wonderful thing."

"Thomas," shouted the professor. "I see you had some visitors while I was gone." Jumping to his feet he replied, "Yes, sir, and I'm afraid they got away with the chemicals."

"Fine, fine, that's just what we wanted them to do. Now that they have, we can put our plan into action."

Confused, Thomas asked, "You mean you knew all along they would come and take what they wanted?"

"Yes, my boy, why do you think we didn't come when you called?"

"Well, I thought maybe something happened to you."

"Nonsense, we're immortal. Nothing can happen to us."

Jonathan looked at his father and said, "What do you mean, you're immortal?"

"My boy, you have so many questions, and I have too little time to explain."

"Well, why not Dad? Have you got a hot date or something?" he laughed.

"My boy, I have a date with destiny," he said as he and the trio vanished.

With an irritated look Jonathan said, "Some things never change. He's still too busy to spend time with his only son." Marian took his hand and tried to explain.

"You have no idea how important your father's work is and why he must do what he has to do; you have to understand."

"Oh, yes, I know how important his work is; I've heard it my entire life. Say, what did he mean he's immortal? How is that possible?"

She closed her eyes for a moment and when they opened she said, "All things are possible, especially the impossible. I have certainly learned that from your father."

On another plane of existence, an invisible Ghost Kitty, while doing surveillance on the shadow entities, learned how they mastered excavating the kyanite crystals. The chemicals produced in the lab gave them the ability to levitate and move the crystals from one location to the other, but their powers were weak. It took several of them at one time to move just a small amount. As he watched he saw one group leave and another one follow. He asked himself, "*Um, I wonder where they're going?*" He decided to tag along.

Much to his surprise they returned to the professor's decompression chamber, where they heated the crystals at extreme temperatures causing them to undergo irreversible expansion and become a solid hard mass. And with just a tiny bit of crystal each one of the entities took possession of the mass and became *The Shadow People*.

They were the same smoke-colored silhouettes with no discernible mouths or noses and glowing red eyes, but they had the ability to hold their form and walk upon the earth. But, they had to remain in darkness, so as not to be discovered, and they fed off the fear of the humanoids. The more fear they could generate, the stronger they became, until they were like an army of thousands.

Ghost Kitty returned to the professor and told him what he had learned. "That's a good boy. That's exactly what we wanted them to do, and now it's time for us to get to work."

Roedee asked, "*But, professor, why have we waited so long while they grow stronger?*"

"Timing, my boy, timing." Roedee was very puzzled and didn't understand. He started to second guess the professor.

"*Midnight,*" he asked. "*Are you sure we're doing the right thing by waiting? I mean those Shadow People are harming a lot of innocents while we just sit around here doing nothing."*

"Roedee, you must trust the professor. Now do what you're told."

And that night their work began, as they traveled to a large city and found themselves in alleys and sewers where the homeless slept and tried to survive. The shadow entities would appear and with the casting of their fiery red eyes upon a victim, they drained the energy out of the weak and left lifeless bodies lying where they once stood. The streets were lined with hundreds of corpses, as though a black plague had fallen upon the city.

This was way outside the boundaries of local police, who were stunned and looked upon the massacre as a way to rid the city of degenerates. But not all homeless were degenerates. They were people just like you and me, trying to endure hard times.

The chase was on. The trio and the professor followed the *Shadow People* from one big city to another and with each victim they attacked, the trio healed them, just before they reached the brink of death. For the hundreds that died, hundreds more were saved, but their fear ran rapid and swept across the country like a fire burning out of control. The homeless could no longer hide, and the fear for their lives ruled their every move. The trio continued to follow the shadow entities from city to city, cleaning up their messes while the professor returned to the lab to destroy the decompression chamber.

"Thomas, my boy. Where are you?" shouted the professor. Not receiving a response, he walked outside and looked down the long stretch of sea shore and saw his faithful lab assistant walking along the beach with a beautiful blonde woman. "Thomas, come my boy, we've got work to do." Unbeknownst to Thomas the woman he entertained on the beach slipped a small listening device in his coat and followed him back to the lab. "Professor, nice to see you. How are you, and where's the trio?" asked Thomas.

"They're saving lives my boy. We must destroy the decompression chamber, and we must do it now. Where is Professor Rutherford?"

"She's in town with Jonathan today assisting with a benefit to help the homeless." "Oh, my, that isn't good. Thomas, you must start to dismantle the decompression chamber. As long as its here the shadow entities will continue to come and they must be stopped. Do you understand?"

"Yes, sir, but…how are you going to prove to the world about your existence, if we destroy the chamber? What if we need to re-clone you?"

"Just do as I tell you, my boy. I must leave and find Jonathan and Marian before it's too late." As the professor exited the building he vanished right before the beautiful blue eyes of Mallory Malone, who could not believe what she was seeing. *So, the professor is a re-creation of himself,* she thought. *I can make millions by revealing his secret and special powers, but who's going to believe me? This is not at all possible, or is it? There has to be a way to make a buck out of this discovery. I've got it; I need to keep Thomas from disassembling the chamber, and then I'll have my proof.*

Chapter 21

Meanwhile, it was just about dusk in Manhattan. Crowds gathered in the streets to partake of a free meal sponsored by several religious organizations and the New York City Mayor. The homeless were fed and collections were taken to provide a much needed place to sleep hundreds of people who had nothing but the clothes on their backs.

As nighttime fell over the city, there was a massive power outage and total darkness covered downtown Manhattan. The fiery red eyes of the *Shadow People* peered upon the crowd, producing great fear and panic as they started to drain their energy. The entities learned that humanoids, other than the homeless, contained greater levels of energy, which made them stronger, so they attacked the weak and the strong.

The professor located Marian and Jonathan and placed a protective shield around them as he called for the trio. "Midnight, hear me now. Bring forth your *Ghost Riders* and save these people." And the trio appeared, chasing away the entities and healing those who had not succumbed fully to the brink of death. Hundreds died but hundreds were saved. This was truly a war between good and evil.

"Dad," shouted Jonathan. "What's going on?" Marian begged him to stay calm, because his fear would attract the entities. "Son, you're safe as long as you stay inside that force field. You must remain calm until we can get things under control."

The professor stopped in his tracks and stated, "Marian, that's it.... if we can calm the general population we can eliminate the entities. Without fear, there is no basis for their survival. Come, we must get to work." The city lights were bright again but corpses of those they could not save lined the streets, leaving behind great sadness and even more fear.

They returned to the lab where they found Mallory Malone, gun in hand, threatening to shoot Thomas if anyone came towards her. "I'll shoot him if you come any closer. The rules are going to change. I'm in charge now and this machine is not going to be destroyed. It's going to be my proof to show the world how.... "

The trio surrounded the insistent woman as their eyes turned fiery red. She dropped the gun and stood frozen.

"My dear, you have no idea of whom or what you're dealing with, so you best take a seat and listen," commanded the professor.

Marian took Jonathan's hand and sat beside him as the professor spoke. "I have learned that all of this is part of an overall plan put together by someone or something greater than you or I, and I know science has brought me back for a reason, but I don't have all the answers. I must employ your help."

"Dad, you know we would do anything to help you. Just tell us what to do," said Jonathan.

"My boy, you can keep yourself safe by remaining calm. Marian you can help me produce a mishmash that will calm the general population, which we will introduce into the water supply. This will give us the advantage we need to conquer these entities.

"But, sir, I'm perplexed. If these are alien life forms, they need to be studied. Why did you allow them to enter through the chamber, only to destroy them now?"

"I don't have the answer my dear, and I don't fully understand it myself. I do know that I believe everything happens for a reason, whether we think it's right or wrong."

By the following morning the professor made a decision. "We will not destroy the decompression chamber. We will instead redesign its purpose and utilize it as a trap to capture the shadow entities. Those that have taken form, and walk upon the earth, will need to be lured back here. We'll do that with the chemicals that drew them here in the first place. We'll need to figure a way to retain them, as their powers have grown very strong. But, in the meantime, we need to contaminate the earth's water supply to keep the general population calm and at peace."

Marian asked, "Professor, how is that possible? We're only a handful of people." "Yes, my dear, but we have the power of an army, and what have I always taught you?" She muttered, "Believe in the impossible because anything is possible."

"That's right, now let's get to work."

Thomas grew more concerned about Telesa, as she still hadn't returned any of his calls. Worried she may have been the victim of the *Shadow People*, he asked Midnight to check on her. Appearing before her in Chiptaw, his stunning black fur glistening in the morning sun; he purrs as she approaches him.

"Midnight, I've been worried about you. I could sense something was wrong. How is Thomas?"

With a faint "*meow*," Midnight twirled around generating a vortex of energy which surrounded Telesa and the next thing she knew, she was back at the lab in Long Island.

"Whoa, where am I?" she asked. At that very moment, Thomas came into the room and caught her as she started to fall. "Telesa, you came back. Oh, honey, I'm so glad to see you. I have missed you so much." Looking somewhat distraught she asked, "Thomas, how did I get here? I was just in Chiptaw."

Midnight spoke, "*Telesa, you will be safer here with us,*" and he vanished.

"Hey, somebody better let me out of here. This is kidnapping," shouted the mouthy blonde.

Recognizing her voice Telesa asked, "So, she's here now, I see. Have you already replaced me Thomas Sheffield?"

He tried to explain, "Honey, you don't understand. Just calm down and let me tell you what's been going on around here."

"I know exactly what's been going on around here and you can't tell me anything I don't already know. Do you hear what I'm saying Thomas Sheffield?" she shouted.

Jonathan and his father entered the room to see what all the commotion was, and Telesa couldn't believe her eyes.

"Is that really you professor?"

"Yes, my dear, it is, and you mustn't be angry with Thomas. That woman means absolutely nothing to him. She was simply trying to blackmail the both of you for money. And now that she's discovered me, she wants to tell the world for her own financial gain. But there are more important matters at hand, and we need your help."

"My help? But, how can I help?"

"You'll see my dear, you'll see, but right now you best forgive your husband. He's been next to impossible since you left." She turned to Thomas and smiled like she hadn't smiled in weeks. They shared a kiss, and reunited their love.

"Now, that's what I'm talkin' about," shouted Roedee as Telesa stared at his little nose twitching in the air.

"A talking mouse?" she asked.

Thomas said, "Yes, we have a lot to tell you... more than you could ever imagine."

"Hey," shouted the boisterous blonde in the back room. "Somebody better let me out of here and right now." Telesa followed the sound and stood before the woman, face to face, and although words were unspoken, plenty was said.

Mallory Malone was released after being forced to drink some of the potion prepared to calm the general population. She was as gentle as a lamb and after being returned to her car, she drove off in silence, without condemnation or vengeance. The potion was so concentrated that only small amounts were needed, so the trio began their mission to dispatch it into the world's water supply. This was not an easy task for the mighty trio, even with their superpowers. But, with persistence their difficult task is accomplished. In the days that followed Thomas and the professor refigured the decompression chamber.

It took some time for the tainted water to take effect, but soon the majority of the world was at peace. A world of chaos was at last in harmony. The plan was to fight evil by doing good. The human race must escape the reality of their own evilness; mankind was just a pawn in the battle to come.

By now the shadow entities were in numbers so great they covered the entire earth. The sun, moon, and stars glowed brighter than ever before, making it difficult for the *Shadow People* to walk upon the earth. They lurked in darkness and came only into the light to capture and drain the energy from their unsuspecting prey. The trio cleaned up behind them, saving those they could and chasing away the evil beings. They became known to the world as Midnight's '*Ghost Riders In The Sky*.'

However, the fury of Mother Nature covered the globe, showing no mercy. Massive storms caused flooding upon a third of the earth. Earthquakes and fires consumed another third and famine tossed the weak into a dark abyss.

The destruction was catastrophic. Title waves covered the shores for hundreds of miles inland, but the lab was spared. Midnight looked at the professor and asked, "*Have the humanoids abandoned all hope?*"

With a smile and a nod the professor announced, "Only the evil doers will fear. By them looking upon their wickedness, they will turn to pillars of salt. And salt, my young friend, is a mineral which the shadow entities must have to survive."

Thomas enters the lab. "Is everyone all right?"

"Yes, my boy, come and help me adjust the electromagnetic fields on the decompression chamber. This will hopefully allow the shadow entities to enter and return from where they came." Sulfur and salt were the primary elements placed inside, so condensed that it could be detected from across nations.

Ghost Kitty had been on an assignment. When he returned he reported his findings to the professor. "*I have seen a vision in the sky. It had a head of gold and a belly of brass. Its chest and arms were made of silver and its legs and feet were made of iron mixed with clay. Was it the ruler of the Shadow People?*"

Marian couldn't believe what she was hearing, but she listened. Ghost Kitty said, "*I then saw a second vision. A beast rose up out of the sea with seven heads and ten horns and on the horns were ten crowns. It looked like a leopard, but it had the feet of a bear and the mouth of a lion. A dragon gave the beast great power; the evil overcame good, and the humanoids worshiped the dragon. How are we going to defeat them?"*

Rodee jumped up and wiggled his tail and shouted, *"We'll defeat those dirtballs, don't you worry."*

"Calm down Roedee," said the professor. "Your time will come to do your part, you must be patient. Seek the truth and the truth will set you free." Marian had to ask, "But, sir, what is the truth?"

The professor, with all his wisdom, replied, "Brotherhood, human heritage, and the ability to reason. We are all searching for the truth my dear, and the meaning of life. These entities are of an ancient energy, which rose to power a thousand years ago. They were technologically advanced on their home planet, until they became wicked and unbelieving and were cast out as shadows. They lived in a bottomless pit, a lake of fire and brimstone and they are an abode of evil spirits. But, they fear the light and with the great light their spirits will be carried away into the wilderness."

After some final adjustments, the decompression chamber was ready. "Thomas, when the trio and I step inside, you must trigger switches two, three, and nine; when the cycle of lights completes its rotation you must again trigger the same switches. You must do this four times, once for each of us. Do you understand?"

"Yes sir, but will you be harmed?"

"You needn't worry my boy, we will be safe. Now get

on with it, time is wasting." And Thomas did just as he was instructed. He triggered the switches and completed the rotation of lights four times, and at the end of the rotation there was a light, so bright they were forced to look away.

"Marian," shouted Thomas. "Do you think they're all right?"

She shook her head and said, "I think they're better than all right." The trio and the professor stepped out of the chamber.

"Professor, what happened?" asked Marian. "It's simple my dear. The trio now has the power of three and with their tri-fold structure they will be the alignment between good and evil. With their ability to become an equilateral triangle they will become symbolic to the human race protecting those who seek the truth. Their journey will take them wherever evil lurks as their destiny unfolds."

The professor and the trio were soon on the trail of the shadow entities, jumping from one dimension to the other. Since the potion placed in the water calmed the general population the *Shadow People* had fewer and fewer victims, but they survived on the pillars of salt of those evildoers who looked upon their own wickedness. They became a feeding ground for ultimate evil.

Dusk was approaching and the trio stationed themselves in the heavens in the shape of a perfect triangle with sulfur and salt placed in the middle. It wasn't long before several of the shadow entities gathered seeking the contents. The trio's collars cast out three rays of magnificent bright light, with each ray meeting in the middle for the ultimate power of annihilation. At that very instant the entities, inside the force field, were destroyed.

"*Yeah, now that's what I'm talking about!*" shouted Roedee as he clicked his heels and jumped in the air.

"*Yeah,*" said Ghost Kitty. "*Come back for more you cowards, if you want a piece of me.*"

Midnight was very pleased as he led the trio on their next mission and then another and another, but the fight had just begun.

CHAPTER 22

More drops of the potion had to be disbursed in the world's water supply, and where the shadows roamed the trio followed, saving those they could from the brink of death. Suddenly bolts of lightning filled the darkened sky, followed by echoes of thunder. Darkness covered the city midday, and the beast appeared. It had a snake-like body with scaly skin, wings sixty feet across, and gigantic claws.

With the eyes of a serpent, it breathed fire. Flames dripped from its lower jaw and the corners of its mouth. It flew over the city generating more fear and panic than the potion could handle, and it came when the trio were their most vulnerable. With its fiery breath and destructive powers it immobilized the city and the *Shadow People* attacked. It was a massacre and the city was destroyed leaving behind the beaten trio.

"*Professor, we need your help,*" cried Midnight. "*We were weakened after healing the humanoids when the beast attacked.*" The professor quickly returned the trio to the lab where they regained their strength.

"My, my, we can't have this happen again," said the professor. "But, I think I have the remedy," he stuttered as he disappeared. He reappeared hours later with a chemical assortment different from any of the others.

"Thomas, my boy, I want you to take this piece of kyanite crystal and this pillar of salt and place it in the decompression chamber, and then close the door and keep your fingers crossed."

"But, why professor?"

"Because, I said so, now get on with it my boy."

"Yes sir," and Thomas did just as he was instructed.

"Marian," summoned the professor. "I need you to inject these chemicals into the decompression chamber exactly when I tell you. Not before or after. It must be exactly when I tell you. Do you understand?"

"Yes, I'm ready." He motioned the trio to take their stance around the chamber forming the perfect equilateral symbol. "Now when I give you the signal each of you must engage your collars. Are we ready?" After getting an affirmative response the plan was put into action.

Thomas placed the kyanite crystals and pillar of salt inside the chamber and closed the door while Marian prepared to inject the chemicals. The trio formed their triangle while the professor hit switches two, three, and nine. As the circle of lights began their rotation the professor shouted, "Now."

The trio cast out three rays of magnificent bright light with each ray meeting in the middle. Suddenly, there was an explosion inside the chamber, and the entire process came to a halt. "That's fine," said the professor as he opened the door to the chamber. All at once the room filled with tiny flying furry creatures.

"*Cool,*" shouted Roedee.

"*What are they?*" asked Midnight.

"These, my little friends, are your fur mates."

"*Say what?*" asked Ghost Kitty.

"They look like furry miniature gargoyles," said Thomas. "You're quite right, my boy. I think we'll call them *Gargyies.* When they're at rest, they will be gigantic stations of stone outside the lab guarding it from the *Shadow People.*"

"Professor," asked Marian. "How is this possible?"

"There you go again my dear. When are you ever going to learn that the impossible is always possible if you only believe?" She shook her head is disbelief and sat down to listen. "They look gnarly all right, but they have special powers to be used against the beast when the trio is weak," said the professor.

"*What kind of special powers?*" asked Midnight.

"Well, the chemicals we injected will give the *gargyies* speed and mobility. Although their bites will not destroy, they will weaken the beast. And if all goes as planned, after enough bites, the beast will no longer destroy, as it will develop empathy for the humans its terrorizing."

"Check it out, man," yelled Roedee.

"Yeah, well they're on my list, so let's get to it," roared Ghost Kitty.

"They will also be your messengers, and you must use them as such. Do you understand?" asked the professor. With the nods of their heads the trio vanished and the *gargyies* followed.

This time, their battle took place over the large lakes of the world known in ancient times as the seven seas. The trio stationed themselves in the heavens above, in the shape of a triangle, with sulfur and salt placed in the middle where the shadows gathered.

The trio's collars cast out three rays of light with each ray meeting in the middle and the entities, inside the force field, were destroyed. The cosmic battle between good and evil was a victory. Their fighting continued and with each battle the beast grew larger and stronger. This time the beast appeared in the ocean as a sea serpent with two snake-like heads, fiery red eyes, and a tail so powerful, it moved its massive body and heads four feet above the waters surface. The trio called the *gargyies* to fight the beast, while they rounded up more of the shadow entities. Then suddenly, a swarm of the furry little creatures surrounded the two heads, nipping and biting the beast until finally it retreated to the depths of the ocean.

Meanwhile, it was discovered that the potion placed in

the world's water supply was no longer calming the general population; once again panic and hysteria covered the planet. The humanoids feared for their lives as they searched for a new world order.

Telesa became very ill and Thomas called the trio to heal her. "Midnight, I need your help. Telesa is very sick and we can't figure out what's wrong with her. Can you do something?" The trio placed their paws upon her as she lay in her weakened state.

With a look of discontentment Midnight meowed and said, *"She has been consumed by evil and we cannot help her."*

Thomas couldn't believe what he was hearing. "But, why? You have saved thousands and thousands. Why can't you save her?"

"I healed her once and I can't do it again. Not even with the power of the trio." Thomas felt abandoned and hopeless. He didn't want to live without her.

At that moment the professor appeared by her bed and placed her hand in his and said, "Remember my dear when you said you wanted to help me and you wondered how?"

"Yes," she mumbled.

"Well, now it's time. You must fight, but more importantly you must believe you will get better. You must see past the pain. Your duty is to honor the responsibility to your spirit and soul. Battle the evil inside you, and your struggle will be victorious, and the reward you receive will be beyond your dreams." And with that thought, she slipped into a coma and slept as she battled the beast inside her.

The trio's crusade carried on. Good against evil. The fight to rule over mankind. Their powers to destroy the

Shadow People grew stronger as did the powers of the shadow entities. It seemed they were an equal match. Their path this time took them to the desert where they stationed themselves high above the sand dunes in the shape of a perfect triangle with sulfur and salt placed in the middle where the shadows gathered. Their collars cast out three rays of magnificent light with each ray meeting in the middle and the entities inside their force field were destroyed.

And the beast appeared again with three snake-like heads, fiery red eyes, and a tail so long that the beast slithered across the desert, breathing fire and destroying all life. The *gargyies* came from the heavens to fight the beast. The furry little creatures surrounded the three heads, nipping and biting the beast until finally it took refuge in the sand.

Their next destination was Paris, France, on top of the Eiffel Tower where they gazed down upon the city. It was just about dusk as they waited for the *Shadow People.* Roedee stood up, wiggled his tail and said, "*Here, lizard, lizard,*" and the beast appeared.

"*Oh, man, I was only kidding,*" said Roedee, and the battle resumed, but this time they were not prepared.

The beast now had four snake-like heads and two sets of wings sixty feet across. Molted rock dripped from its powerful jaws and claws as it flew over the city, generating fear and horror among the humanoids, spitting and sputtering fire. The *gargyies* immediately surrounded the trio and turned into gigantic stations of stone gargoyles that the beast feared. From their mouths a powerful water-spout emerged and doused the flames.

Another group of *gargyies* attacked the beast, nipping and biting until the beast finally succumbed and vanished, but not before the shadow entities sucked the energy out of thousands of humanoids, and it was too late for the trio to save them.

They returned to the lab and reported to the professor. Midnight scolded Roedee. "*This is not a game Roedee. This is serious and needs your full attention.*"

"*But, Midnight, it was just a joke. I was only kidding.*" Roedee was left alone to think about what he had done.

"*It wasn't my fault. How did I know the beast would come if I called him?*" Ghost Kitty tried to comfort his little friend.

"*You don't understand do you Roedee?*"

"*Understand what?*"

"*Midnight tried to explain to you about how serious this is, and you keep cracking jokes.*"

"*Yeah, well, whatever.*"

"*Look little mouse,*" growled Ghost Kitty. "*You're long overdue for an attitude adjustment.*"

"*Yeah, well, don't even think about it,*" shouted the courageous rodent.

Meanwhile, the news of the beast and the *Shadow People* reached all corners of the earth. Nations joined together in an attempt to overcome this invasion of evil. Many heard rumors about *Midnight's Ghost Riders*, but they found it hard to believe. Whoever heard of animals with superhero powers? Why it was utterly ridiculous. The weak were still getting attacked. It was decided the shadow entities were extraterrestrial beings from another world. They had no clue on how to fight them; much less, how to destroy them.

"Professor, we need more help," insisted Midnight. *"Their powers are equal to ours and the beast is becoming stronger. There has to be more we can do to overcome their evil."* The professors' response was, "You know what to do my friend, and you have the power with the trio to vanquish your enemies. You must find balance in this unbalanced world. This is your test of obedience. Just remember the beast will look like a lamb, but speak like a dragon; the beast will pull fire from the sky and perform miracles under the false pretense of peace. The sun will shine willingly upon you and give you light. Now go and do what you must do."

Nothing further was said as Midnight joined the trio over the great pyramids of Giza. These remnants of ancient Egypt were an awesome sight, standing strong and hence, Midnight and his brothers found strength in the pyramids overlooking the Nile Valley. Their triangular shape and design presented a parallel universe and intensified their ability to form the perfect equilateral triangle. They found comfort and energy in the pyramids where pharaohs slept in their tombs of stone. The trio would often return to this safe haven to regain their power.

Mallory Malone stayed in New York trying to make connections with some of the nations leaders. She had a story to sell, but no one believed her, as she had no proof. She wanted money, lots of money, and in order to get the proof she demanded payment. But that wasn't going to happen. At least not this way.

Ghost Kitty came to her and tried to reason with her, but she paid him little mind. Angrily, he shouted, "*You will be destroyed by the Shadow People just like every other humanoid. I can save you, but you must pay the price.*" She had no idea just how true the cat's statement was going to be as she ventured into the darkness and was besieged by the shadow entities. Ghost Kitty called on the *gargyies* to follow and protect her.

The furry little creatures flew all around her without being seen, and they acted as spies. She managed to hold back her fear so that the shadow entities would have no reason to attack. "Take me to your leader, I have a proposal." Through telepathy the shadow entities spoke with her, wanting to know just what it was she had to offer. She refused to answer unless she spoke to someone in authority. All at once she and the unseen *gargyies* were transported to another dimension where she stood before a winged lion with birdlike feet looking gnarly and brutish. It screeched with a cry so loud and tormented that it seemed forever lost as it hovered over the lake of fire.

She passed through the lake of fire unscathed and came upon the beast, half man with several heads and one body. She hid her fear as she spoke with the beast. "You must take the form of a human and through the leaders of all the nations you must create a New World Order using peace as a weapon and through peace you will possess many."

She had no idea where these words were coming from; they just rolled out of her mouth. It was as though she were being controlled by some evil spirit, who lead her into the presence of the beast. Her reward, a wealth greater than she had ever known. She was returned from whence she came, delighted in knowing she was going to be very, very rich. Nothing else mattered. The *gargyies* returned to the lab and informed the trio and the professor and preparations were made for the final battle.

Telesa had awakened from her coma as Thomas embraced her and said, "Honey, are you alright? I've missed you." Suddenly her eyes turned from a deep sapphire blue to a fiery red and Thomas was cast across the room. The trio appeared and fought the evil inside her as she kept inflicting injury on Thomas, scratching his chest and arms. She shouted, "The sun will turn to darkness and the moon to blood and the world will be absorbed by fire and billows of smoke." She collapsed, falling back into unconsciousness.

"*Thomas, are you alright?*" asked Midnight. Marian treated his wounds, as the trio vanished, taking refuge over the great pyramids of Giza, where the professor joined them. With the wisdom of a prophet the professor explained, "The vision seen by Ghost Kitty is about to come forth and we must be prepared. The beast will rise up and all the world will worship him and give him power. He will promise peace with the *Shadow People* but peace will never come to pass. He will pull fire from the sky and perform miracles to deceive the humanoids and those who listen and wear his mark will be destroyed, along with the shadow entities. The time is near and only the most righteous of mankind will survive.

Chapter 23

Once again, Mother Nature's fury covered the globe. Earthquakes and storms so great and furious, passed over cities, leaving them without power, clean water, or food. Masses of people were left desperate, crying for help but no one cared. Leaders of nations lost control and with the devastation they feared the existence of mankind was about to come to an end.

Then a man appeared from a foggy mist dressed in a white suit representing compassion and hope. He stood before the great leaders of many nations and he spoke, "I am the comforter and I can save the world from its destruction."

As he spoke the sun turned dark and blood coated the

moon. Fire and billows of smoke surrounded the man who claimed to be the world's redeemer. With that fire, he cast a blazing inferno high in the sky, and the moon turned white again, the sun rose, and a new day was born. Water, food, and electrical power were restored. A feeling of salvation circled the globe and the leaders rejoiced, giving praise to the comforter.

"I have the answer to saving mankind from the extraterrestrial beings who have invaded the earth. I can restore all nations, we will become a New World Order. Do I have the support of the people?" asked the false messenger. And the leaders gave praise to the comforter and agreed to make him ruler of the new world order

"I am *Nebo Zorah*, and I can destroy all wickedness and protect the innocents." He kept his promises and restored order world wide. But not all people believed in him. Many refused to worship him, so he passed a law to destroy those who failed to accept him as ruler of the new world.

The trio came upon the world's longest suspension bridge, The Golden Gate Bridge. They positioned themselves high above in the shape of a triangle with sulfur and salt placed in the middle where the shadows gathered.

Their collars cast out three rays of brilliant white light with each ray meeting in the middle and the entities inside their force field were destroyed. And the beast appeared with five snake-like heads and two sets of wings sixty feet across, flying low over the city, spitting fire and the *gargyies* attacked nipping and biting the beast until it retreated into the sewers below the city.

"*Now that's what I'm talking about*," shouted Roedee.

Next they appeared at *Stonehenge* and Roedee had many questions about this strange place. "*Check it out man. What is this thing?*" he asked.

"*It is thought to be a temple of worship for ancient earth,*" relayed Midnight.

"*Well, what's it purpose now?*"

"*You ask too many questions Roedee,*" said Ghost Kitty.

"*Oh shutinzeup jerk-face,*" yelled the little mouse.

"*Quit fooling around and let's get to work,*" ordered Midnight.

Once again they formed the perfect triangle high in the sky and the shadow entities came and they were destroyed. "*Will we ever be able to destroy them all?*" asked Roedee. "*Not at this pace,*" said Midnight and they returned to the great pyramids where they rested and re-energized.

The *gargyies* were doing their best, acting as spies, watching everything *Zorah* was doing and reporting back to the professor, who had a serious discussion with the trio. "Lads, I have learned much about this *Nebo Zorah*. In ancient times his name *Nebo* meant he spoke of things to come, like the future, but his name *Zorah* means he is a scab, a leprosy, and he must be destroyed along with the shadow entities."

"The innocents who refuse to worship him and wear his mark are destined for destruction and only we can save them, but we must do so on a much larger scale. We must set a trap to lure the shadow entities and *Zorah* to a place where they can be destroyed and the decompression chamber is the key."

Suddenly the beast appeared over the pyramids of Giza

but this time he had transformed into a dragon with one large head and wings seventy feet across. His eyes were no longer fiery red but blue as the ocean and he spoke to the trio. "I come in peace to help you fight the *Shadow People*," he said as he lowered his head. "I feel great shame for the harm I have caused mankind and I want to do my part to help. Please tell me what I can do?"

The professor sent a telepathic message to the trio. "Well, what do you know the empathy juice finally worked."

The dragon spoke again, "There is another beast much like me, but I can protect you." Roedee jumped up and said, "*Why should we trust you, dragon?*" Tears flooded the eyes of the remorseful creature as did Roedee's. The *gargyies* circled the dragon as did the trio.

"*Well, do we destroy him?*" asked Ghost Kitty.

"*No, he is one of us now,*" said Midnight.

Now that the professor knew the empathy juice was working, he sent the *gargyies* to Boston to visit his daughter, Tasha Marie, where they injected her repeatedly and returned to the professor confirming their mission had been accomplished. "Fine, fine, that will keep her safe from the *Shadow People* until we can defeat them and maybe, just maybe, get her off her high society soap box," he laughed.

The *gargyies* next deed was to inject Mallory Malone and, of course, they were successful. The professor ordered everyone to return to the lab as he had new plans to destroy the shadow entities.

"Thomas, how is Telesa?" asked the professor. "She's still fighting sir. I hope she's strong enough to beat this thing."

"She will, my boy, she will. Come and help me with

the decompression chamber. I want to recalculate the settings for time travel."

"Time travel?" he asked. "Yes, my boy, time travel. This machine brought in those shadow entities and by golly it can take them out."

"But, how professor?"

"How, isn't the question lad, but when."

After making several adjustments the new plan was put into place.

"Midnight," shouted the professor. "Summon your *Ghost Riders* and prepare to take a ride back in time."

"To where professor?"

"To the very beginning before mankind came to exist."

"But, why? What's the purpose?" asked Ghost Kitty.

"You must find the portal where the entities came through so we can send them back."

"Hey, can we take the dragon?" asked Roedee.

"No," said the professor. "Now get going." And while they were gone the dragon kept a watchful eye on the *Shadow People* and *Zorah*.

With the help of modern technology and his super powers, the professor constructed a transparent prison in the shape of a pyramid, which would detain the shadow entities until the time of their destruction. The trio will collect them by the thousands by luring them into the decompression chamber. Once gathered, they will be transported to the prison.

The pyramid dungeon will sit high above Giza, unseen by human eyes with a force field so powerful the entities dare not consider crossing it or they will suffer the torment of eternal punishment. During the trio's travel back in time, they learned many lessons and they understood the secret of humanity. They yearned to become sons of man and have the gifts that only the highest power could bestow upon mankind, the gift of a human spirit and soul. Once the evil doers are captured, the trio will cast out a great bright light, and vanquish them forever.

The trap was set to start capturing the shadow entities by placing sulfur and salt inside the decompression chamber, and as the entities were captured, they were transported to the pyramid prison.

The trio kept on battling the entities, saving those they could. This time they found themselves on the top of Mount Everest, a mountain of rock and snow in the Himalayas, where few men have ventured and survived. Dragon was right there with them when the second beast appeared from beneath the snow capped mountain. It had six snake-like heads and three sets of wings, sixty feet across; from its claws and jaws dripped molted rock. Its eyes were fiery red and projected flames, which pierced the skin of the dragon, but the dragon fought back.

The *gargyies* attacked, nipping and biting the beast until it finally retreated beneath the snow. But the beast appeared again in the largest gorge in the world—two hundred and ninety miles long, setting fires and destroying everything in its path. The trio followed and positioned themselves high above, in the shape of a perfect triangle. Their collars cast out three rays of bright light, each ray meeting in the middle and the beast was destroyed. "*Yes,*" said Roedee, "*now that's what I'm talkin' about.*" They were victorious.

As darkness approached, Mallory Malone sat quietly in her room wondering about what Ghost Kitty said, *I can save you but you must pay the price.* For the first time in a long time, she recognized that her chosen path would cost her more than any amount of riches could ever buy. She was overcome with a feeling of warmth and compassion. She felt goodness in her heart, which was something she lost many, many years ago. The reality of the world was upon her, and she felt responsible for the take over by *Zorah*. She had to do what she did best, and pull off the con of the century by trapping *Zorah*—it wouldn't be easy.

The trio proceeded with their round up of the shadow entities containing over ninety percent, but the battle was far from over. They concentrated more on protecting the innocents who protested wearing the mark of *Zorah*. The pure at heart became weak and frail as they resisted the laws of *Zorah*.

Mallory Malone witnessed their persecution. She had to do something fast, as she hadn't yet taken the mark of *Zorah* and she, was at risk. "Ghost Kitty, if you can hear me, please come. I need your help, please come," she screamed. And moments later the white cat appeared.

"*I'm here humanoid. What do you want?*"

She started to cry, which softened Ghost Kitty. "Tell

me, what is the price I must pay for you to save me? I'll do anything," she begged.

"You must be willing to give of yourself and you will be saved." She struggled to understand.

"Do you mean I have to do good deeds? That's no problem, I can do whatever you want me to."

Ghost Kitty meowed and fluttered his eyes and said, *"You must give yourself if you want to be saved,"* and he vanished. She thought passionately about his words, but she still didn't understand. Then it hit her, and she knew exactly what she needed to do.

The witching hour drew closer, as she made her way to see *Zorah*. As she entered his presence, she could feel the magnetism of this false comforter and she was drawn to him. She fought the obsession with all her might, and while doing so she found great strength deep within. The *gargyies* acted as her protector and unbeknownst to her they proceeded to biting and nipping *Zorah* with their mighty empathy juice, and after a period of time *Zorah's* power seemed to weaken. Mallory was no longer afraid and she spoke, "*Zorah*, I come to you with another proposition. What is it that you want most?"

He studied her long and hard before he answered, "Destruction of the trio, worship and praise as the ruler of the New World Order."

She smiled and nodded her head which made him all the more curious. "What if I can deliver them all? What's it worth to you?"

He gazed at her with his penetrating dark eyes and asked, "What's it worth to you Mallory Malone? I don't see you wearing my mark. Why shouldn't I destroy you right now?"

She laughed and said, "Because you'll never find the trio or the man behind their creation." *Zorah* stared through her as she tried to hide her fear, his wickedness strived to consume her.

"You know the creator?" he asked. "I not only know him, I can deliver him to you for a price."

He agreed and said, "I'll spare your life and give you a fortune greater than you can imagine, if you deliver the trio and their creator." The deal was made and she was allowed to leave.

Chapter 24

The following morning Jonathan was working in his office in Manhattan when he received a call from Tasha. "Hello Brother, how are you? My goodness, have you been listening to the news about everything going on in the world?" He was glad to hear she was safe.

"Yes I have, and how are you and your family?"

He sensed the worry in her voice. "Well, it hasn't been easy but we've been able to manage. Say, what do you think is going to come of this New World ruler? Can this really be happening?"

Jonathan reassured her everything would be all right just as long as she didn't take his mark. "Brother, I just want you to know, I have always loved you." She was frightened, very frightened and he saw a side of his sister he had long forgotten.

Back at the lab the professor was putting together a synthetic combination of empathy juice as a way to save those who had taken upon them the mark of *Zorah*. Otherwise, they would be destroyed when the time came to eradicate the invaders. He knew he couldn't save them all, but saving even one life was just as important.

"Marian, we can manufacture a synthetic form of the empathy juice but it has to be injected in order to be effective. Do you have any suggestions on how we can do this on a wide scale?"

This theory was the most outrageous one she'd heard yet, even after everything she'd been through. After all she's seen and experienced, she still questioned, "How is this possible?"

Thomas said, "Ye of little faith, Marian. Why is it so hard for you to believe?"

There was a knock at the door, Thomas answered. There stood Mallory Malone. "Thomas, please let me see the professor. It's very important. It's about *Zorah*." Reluctantly, he let her in and took her to see the professor.

"Mallory, my dear, how are you?" he asked as he called the trio. "Please, you must listen. I can help you end this now, if you'll only trust me."

Thomas stood between them and asked, "How can you expect us to trust you after all you've done?"

"I'm so sorry for trying to con you, but I really need your help and I can help you." Thomas asked, "And just how much is this gonna cost?"

"Not one red cent." She begged the professor to listen.

"Sir, I can help you trap *Zorah*. I don't know exactly how, but I know I can. Won't you please let me try?"

The trio took the position of a perfect triangle and prepared to set their collars aglow when the professor said, "Wait, I believe her. Perhaps she can help us." She cried, "I'll do whatever is needed to put an end to that so called comforter."

The professor placed his hand against her cheek and told her, "*Zorah* will destroy you if he finds out. Do you fully understand what that means? Are you willing to accept the consequences?"

She raised her head and with great pride she said, "Yes." At that moment, a bright light fell upon her and lifted her in the air and she felt a peace she had never known before; then it was over.

"So, let's discuss our options," said the professor. "We have captured ninety percent of the *Shadow People* and they are being held prisoner. Because their numbers have dwindled, so have the powers of the comforter. We need to seize the remaining ten percent and somehow inject the empathy juice into those who have accepted his mark. Any thoughts on how we can do this?"

The room grew quiet as they studied the challenge and Mallory exclaimed, "We'll get *Zorah* to inject his people without him knowing that's what he's doing. I mean after all, he's their ruler, so who would be the better man, pardon the pun, to order it done?"

"What an interesting concept," said the professor. "And just how might we do this, Ms. Malone?"

"We'll con him by convincing him it's his only way to gain full control. We'll convince him that his people will never turn away if he injects them just once."

Thomas asked, "But, how do we get him the empathy juice and convince him to use it?"

Mallory boasted, "Leave that to me. I've already set the foundation. Professor, he knows you're the creator of the trio and he wants to have power over you more than anything else. He wants your soul but you don't have one, right?"

"Yes, that's right."

"Then he can't harm you."

Marian said, "We can alter the empathy juice just enough so that when he injects the people they will appear to worship him."

"But Marian," asked the professor, "do you think that's possible?"

"I knew you'd come around. Come now, let's get to work."

They spent all night getting the mishmash to the exact level altering the empathy juice, just slightly with an ego booster. Then they tested it on Telesa who was still in a comatose state fighting the evil inside her.

Thomas stood by patiently as the professor gave her an injection, but she didn't respond. He gave her a second injection and looked at Thomas and said, "Don't worry my boy; she'll come through this just fine." At that moment she opened her eyes and while trying hard to focus she spoke the words, "Hail to *Zorah*." The experiment was a success and she was finally free from the evil inside her.

"Oh, Thomas," she cried as they embraced. "Welcome back, honey."

Rodee was so excited he jumped up and said, "*Now that's what I'm talking about*" and everyone laughed.

Then he shouted, "*Come on dragon, we've got work to do.*" The trio vanished to capture the remaining *Shadow People* while the professor and Mallory made a visit to *Zorah*. Of course the *gargyies* were always somewhere nearby.

They entered *Zorah's* headquarters located in a high rise building on the west end of town. Mallory could sense a change in the way she felt from the last time she was there. She didn't feel threatened or intimidated.

"Professor, you must let me do the talking, okay?"

"Of course, my dear, I'll follow your lead."

Zorah approached them and as soon as he saw the professor, he knew he was the creator. His piercing dark eyes penetrated deep into the chest of the professor and reflected off his mechanical heart. No words were spoken. Only glances were exchanged. Mallory finally broke the silence. "*Zorah*, I have brought you the creator."

Continuing with his penetrating stare he asked, "Is he human?"

She responded, "Yes, he's human."

"Then why does the blood that flows through his veins flow backwards?"

She had no answer, but the professor was quick to respond. "Because *I Left My Heart In San Francisco*," he laughed. Mallory started to laugh and since laughter was so contagious *Zorah* started to laugh. Of course the nipping and biting by the unseen *gargyies* wasn't hurting things either.

The professor explained, "I have a mechanical heart after my human heart gave out because I didn't take care of it the way I should have. But, with this handy little device I invented, I'm just as good as new." Of course "good" was the key word.

"You are a great man Creator…" *Zorah* started.

An agitated Mallory interrupted, "Hey he's here because of our deal. My life in exchange for his soul. Once you have him, you have the trio. But, I have something else that may be of interest to you, but it will cost you dearly."

Zorah looked her way and challenged her, "What could you possibly have that would interest me?" She said with confidence. "A potion designed by the creator to take control of mankind, but something went wrong and the experiment failed. It forces man to commit to evil. But it must be injected before the sun rises tomorrow or it will loose its potency."

Even for an extraterrestrial this sounded pretty far fetched.

"Why should I believe you?" he asked.

"I'll prove it," she said as she took a vial and injected the professor.

"Hail to *Zorah*," the creator spoke. "There, you see. Now he's your pawn to do with as you wish. Now give me my freedom and the money you promised. There's enough potion to inject everyone, but only I know its location. You might say it's my life insurance."

Zorah wasn't convinced. "How do I know this isn't a trap?" he asked.

Mallory handed him another vial and said, "Here, inject whoever you want, except me." He called for the guards to bring him one of the righteous who refused his mark and he injected the human.

Within moments he heard, "Hail *Zorah*," as the human who once defied him now succumbed.

"Fine, but what happens to those who have already accepted me as their comforter?" he asked. Mallory, with a smirk, handed him another vial and said, "Inject one and find out." And so he did and again he heard, "Hail *Zorah*."

He ordered the guards to take the professor to a holding cell as he started the process of injecting all the people in the city. As Mallory brought him more empathy juice, more and more people were getting injected around the world. By morning, the mission was complete and *Zorah* wasn't any bit wiser. Absorbed in his glory and believing he had his enemy right where he wanted, he ordered, "Creator, summon the trio and destroy them."

He did just as he was asked and called the trio. They stationed themselves in the shape of a perfect triangle while their collars cast out three rays of magnificent white light. The professor engaged his ankle bracelet and united with the trio giving them even greater power.

Zorah was trapped inside their force field and transported to the pyramid prison. The final battle was upon them as the night sky filled with swirls of brilliant rays of light that formed into atoms and solar gases. The pyramid prison began to open as the atoms and solar gases turned into a stream of electrically charged particles and the northern sky was covered with ripples and swirls of beaming light. The trio, still in position, expelled all the energy they had collected from the great pyramids. The *Shadow People* were cast into a bottomless pit, a lake of fire and brimstone. And the enemy was vanquished.

At that moment, a light more brilliant and whiter than any light produced by the trio, lit up the heavens and surrounded them and from the light came these words.

"*I am the alpha and the omega, the ruler of all. I am the creator, the eternal most high. I breathe life into the darkness, and into each of you. The light shines willingly upon you, for you have saved mankind from its own destruction. You have protected the innocents and freed the souls of many; you have condemned the evil spirits. You have done well, my sons and the power of your love for mankind has earned you a place in my kingdom. I will grant you that which you seek most, a living soul but you must surrender your immortality and live out your worldly lives as mortal beings. I bless the trio with nine lives and your superpowers should you choose to keep watch over mankind.*"

With the nods of their heads they generously accepted their reward. "*Go now, you're time will come to be with me. Just remember 'You'll Never Walk Alone.'* And they changed in the twinkling of an eye.

Back at the lab, the professor appeared along with the trio as they sat around and discussed their future.

"*Professor?*" asked Midnight. "*What will come of us now that we are mortal?*"

"It's our choice. We have been given a most wonderful gift above all other gifts. We must decide what our future holds."

"Well, what's so great about being mortal?" asked Ghost Kitty.

"With mortality your soul will live forever," explained the professor.

"Well, isn't that the same as being immortal?"

"No, Ghost Kitty, one day you will know death but in death, you'll have everlasting life."

Not fully understanding this conversation Roedee yells, *"Yeah, now that's what I'm talkin' about."*

The professor continued. "Lads, we each have our free agency to make a choice. My choice is to relinquish my immortality and spend my remaining years with my family. I have been given a second chance at life and I choose my family. But, I will always be here if you need me."

All at once the *gargyies* and the *dragon* appeared. The professor explained, "Should you choose to continue to protect the innocents you have been promised you will retain your superpowers but you will still be mortal so you must be cautious in your endeavors. You will face many challenges and you must be prepared. The *gargyies* and the *dragon* will protect you. Each of you have the right to make your own choice."

They took the form of a perfect triangle and as their collars glowed they cast out three rays of magnificent white light with each ray meeting in the middle for the ultimate power.

They recited together, *"We choose to protect the innocents for the rest of our worldly lives."* Then suddenly in the flash of a brilliant light they vanished.

Chapter 25

The trio's next destination was the Caribbean in the Western Hemisphere. The sea's deepest point, the Cayman Trough, is where Captain Cyrus Bohannon, also known as Captain Bo is found sailing his vessel with a crew of seventy rugged men, which he recruited from the lowest of degenerates, forgotten by society. Men who had nothing to lose, who'd do anything to survive. They were promised great fortune and all the rum they could drink if they agreed to sail the seven seas with Captain Bo.

But, there was something very unique about this captain's craft; it was a *pirate ship* right out of the 1700's. She stood strong with three masts and a full suit of square-rigged sails.

Her fore-and-aft mainsail could take wind from both sides. Her foresail and jib had canvas so strong it could endure all the elements and take on the heaviest of rain, wind, and salt. She was indeed a beauty to behold, a most seaworthy vessel, and she went by the name of "*Dark Lady*."

She also bore a secret cloaking device which enabled her to vanish while being pursued by the legal authorities. Fourteen cannons mounted her gun deck and along with their primitive pirate weapons, was all the artillery they needed. They were truly pirates right out of the 1700's who turned to a life of piracy.

Their multi-colored fabrics were often mismatched and worn tightly so as not to interfere with their climbing and rigging. They wore linen shirts, breeches, and stockings, just like the garb worn by pirates of long ago. Some wore black leather boots unless they were swabbing the deck in which case they went barefoot so as not to slip and be injured.

The Captain, dressed in a frock coat and breeches made of rich crimson velvet, flaunted a tri-cornered hat with exotic red and blue feathers. A diagonal satin and leather sash decorated the front of his coat, and the sash around his waist was positioned in such a way so as to hold his weapons of a dagger and pistol. The black leather bucket boots and wide belt around his waist held his curved cutlass sword making his look of a Pirate Captain almost complete. And he wore as much gold and silver as he could muster, representing his great wealth and success as a pirate.

His first mate, Bartholomew Reddick, known as "Red-Eye Jack" from the deep scar across his face, from a fight with a dagger, was the Captains second in command should the Captain be engaged in other matters.

As dawn approached the Captain stood beneath the mainmast and muttered, "I be lettin' ye know tha'since ye be me crew, we'll scour the seven sea's for treasure mates and ye swabs can have all the grog you can drink. Arrrrr.... we'll steal the best booty and hornswaggle our way to bein' the richest pirates on the sea."

The cry from the men was a loud, "Aye, Cap'N Bo."

Red-Eye Jack stood next to the Captain and ordered, "Stop ye whining ye yellow bellied lily-livered landlubbers and grab them sails there mates."

And off they sailed towards Mosquito Lagoon exceeding eleven knots in the right conditions. The approach to the cove was treacherous ringed by shoals and large coral reefs. But over the many months at sea the crew experienced scores of such coves and the navigator was precise in his predictions of the reefs. They lowered the anchor one mile out and boarded the cockboat for shore.

"Avast Cap'n," shouted the first mate. "We be makin' landfall for these lily-livered landlubbers. What say ye Cap'n?"

As he scratched his scraggily grey beard he growled, "We be gettin' supplies mates and I be gettin' me a new parrot."

They stepped onto the sandy beach and entered a huge tropical forest. The Captain picked out the parrot he wanted and ordered his men, "Ye be hookin' me up with tha' there red and blue bird, what say ye mates?"

"Aye, Cap'N," and the chase began, running through

the dense forest with their swords in the air shouting, "Arrrr, Arrrr."

They surrounded the parrot and took him hostage returning him to the Captain for their just reward.

"Well, shiver me timbers, me didn't think you could do such a masterful feat and I be very pleased. Red-Eye Jack, give the mates a night of relaxation. They be goin' to town to partake of grog and wenches. A finer group of pirates thar' never was I say. I'll name me parrot *Sea Dog*, after me once favorite mangy mutt."

Red-Eye Jack ordered, "Be back by dawn you scally-wags and don't be forgettin' yer supplies, Arrrr."

The Captain decided to make his way into the quaint little village following behind his men with *Sea Dog* mounted on his shoulder. He and his crew were immediately noticed in their pirate gear and by the way they spoke. Townsfolk thought they were a traveling minstrel show so they laughed, clapped their hands, and tossed coins their way.

"Arrrr," shouted the men. "Warin' might we find yer tavern and beautiful wenches?"

The crowd crew larger and the more they interacted with the pirates the more the people came to trust them, so they thought.

"Yargh," said the Captain. "I be Cap'N Bo of the *Dark Lady* and we be anchored just outside yer coastline."

The Captain pulled his sword and pistol as his men followed suit.

"We be takin' yer valuables from yer now. Consider it a contribution to our cause, Arrrr."

Then one after the other the pirates robbed each of the towns people leaving them penniless and in shock. They grabbed their supplies as well, free for the taking.

Little did the men know but they were followed back to the ship by a young lass who favored the excitement and unbeknownst to them she came on board as a stole away.

Red-Eye Jack ordered, "Ye scurvy scallywags drag yer sorry keesters on board and hoist them sails. We be get-tin' out of here ye swabs."

The sails were raised and the ship made her exit from the cove out into the open sea. They were moving along at ten knots when they were approached by a large ship, a Coast Guard Ship.

The Captain mumbled, "Ya mangy cockroaches, get them thar'cannons ready to fire, we be overtakin' by a strange lookin' vessel."

The cannons were loaded and filled with powder and upon command of the Captain seven cannons fired, their cannon balls hurled through the air and landed in the sea just shy of the other ship.

"Ye mangy swabs, how be it yer miss yer target?" yelled the Captain. "Yer no better than a whining wench. What say ye?"

The crew answered, "Aye, Cap'N," as they loaded the cannons for another round this time striking the bow of the other ship.

They heard over a loud speaker, "Surrender your ship. You are all under arrest."

All at once the Captain grinned and said, "We not be

given' in to the likes of you," as he engaged the cloaking device and the *Dark Lady* vanished.

Their next stop was Barbados partially enclosed by reefs on the eastern and southern shores surrounded by a turquoise sea. On the north side small coral and sandstone cliffs rise and fall with the coming and going of the tide. Its sandy white beaches at sunset make Barbados one of the most beautiful of all the islands in the Caribbean.

But of greater interest to the Captain was the endless supply of tourist hungry for adventure and the pirates fit right in with the people of Barbados who stood on the streets selling their goods. The crew gathered in front of the vendors as the Captain made the introductions.

"A good afternoon to all ye fine landlubbers. Me and me men be here to entertain you."

The crew shouted a loud, "Aye, Cap'n Bo."

"This be me first mate Red-Eye Jack and he be one the toughest swabs aboard me ship."

The Captain drew his sword and said to the growing crowd, "Look at me new sword. She be a real beauty made of the finest steel and she be slashin' the biggest of men."

Another loud cry came from the crew, "Aye Cap'N," as they pulled their swords and pistols and started firing in the air.

The crowd was intrigued as they watched and listened and threw coins. Red-Eye Jack raised his sword and announced, "We be takin' yer booty now ye lily-livered landlubbers. Smartly there, pirates," as they quickly gathered the treasures and headed for the seashore leaving behind a stunned and angry crowd.

Meanwhile the stole away wondered the ship while the pirates were gone and made herself most comfortable. A little too comfortable as she was found basking in the sun after living many days below deck in the cold and dreary bilge, sneaking out for food and water.

"Avast ye bawcocky sea mates," said the Captain.

"What hav' we here lads but a buxom blonde haired beauty?"

When she woke she was surrounded by the faces of scraggly pirates, but she didn't panic.

"Don't ye worry little one, me crew wants only to behold yer beauty."

They growled, "Aye, Cap'N" as they helped the young lass to her feet.

The Captain approached her with *Sea Dog* on his shoulder. "What say ye wench?" asked the parrot.

Much to the Captain's surprise she answered, "I say I be here to join yer shipmates and sail the seven seas with yer and ye crew Cap'N."

He scratched his beard and mumbled, "Well, shiver me timbers. You be the most pleasin' lookin' wench me eyes ever did see. C'mere me beauty."

She cautiously approached him and growled, "I be from Davy Jones locker where the souls of drowned pirates live and I be reborn to sail on the *Dark Lady*."

Laughter of the crew echoed around the ship, "Har, har, har," hearing such foolish words from such a young girl who was actually a woman full of grit and gumption.

She grabbed the pistol from Red-Eye Jack and ordered, "C'mere ye pirates, its time to fight to yer death.

I be stayin' on board and if any of ye swabs get in me way, I be makin' yer walk the plank, I will."

And the laughter continued, "Har, har, har," as she grabbed a rope from the mainsail and swept over the pirates landing on the main deck.

Red-Eye Jack mumbled, "She's got a fiery disposition, Cap'N."

There was no doubt that this headstrong independent woman, who was fearsomely courageous, was ever going to leave the ship. The Captain respected her temperament and more importantly he loved her at first sight.

"You be an unpredictable lass me lady. What might be yer name lovely one?" asked Captain Bo. Finally at a loss for words, her silence showed signs of fear.

"Tie that dawg to the yardarm," hollered Red-Eye Jack.

Her silence ended when she boasted, "Me'n'these here mangy swabs can bring yer a fortune greater than any the seven seas has ever seen."

From the shoulder of Captain Bo *Sea Dog* cried, "Bawk... bawk... show me the treasures... show me the treasures... pretty one."

The Captain nodded his head and said, "Aye, show me the treasures pretty one."

Taking the rope again from the mainsail she floated over the heads of the crew and landed next to Captain Bo. She looked into his dark brown eyes and bragged, "Me know a way to capture a gigantic ship a thousand times bigger than the *Dark Lady* and rob the sea voyaging guests of their money and jewels and anything else yer fancy valuable."

The Captain was enchanted by this young lass of twenty years and even though it was well-known that having a woman on board a pirate ship was bad luck he decided to go against everything he believed in and allow her to remain.

"Yargh," howled the Captain. "Grog for all ye scallywags. This wench she be stayin' on the *Dark Lady* and she be goin' by the name of *Grace The Temptress* and ye bully boys best leave 'er alone lessin' yer wantin' to deal with me, Arrr."

Red-Eye Jack barked, "Hoist them sails, ye mangy sea rats. We be headin' for Dragons' Island. What see ye in the crows nest and be smartly 'bout it yer scallywag."

The mate answered, "We be gettin'in deep waters mate."

Captain Bo took Lady Grace to the quarterdeck where he snarled, "What be the fathoms?"

The mate answered, "We be at two hundred fathoms Cap'N."

"Arrr, keep her on course. Me'n the beauty be goin' below deck."

She followed him to his quarters where he presented her with a purple velvet double lace up corset and black breeches and thigh high black boots. He placed a red sash around her waist positioned in such a way as to hold a silvery cutless sword. And then to complete her outfit, he placed a black swashbuckler hat with an ostrich feather on her head and said, "Ye be a real pirate now me Lady," as he bowed and took her hand and kissed it ever so gently. He then placed golden chains around her neck and rings on her fingers to represent her worthiness to the crew and she wore a set of pure gold earrings which dangled one inch below each ear.

"Arrr, ye be me buxom beauty."

She was very pleased. Her dreams of adventure were coming true and it was far greater than she had ever imagined.

Captain Bo sat down and summoned the wench, "Aye, c'mere me beauty and tell me of yer plan to capture the gigantic ship."

She sauntered over next to him and started to explain. "It be an easy task Cap'N. We be hijackin' a cruise ship. Yer crew can cast yer ropes and climb on board and take whatever yer fancy. The sea voyaging guest will think it's a special show but we be stealin' 'em blind."

"Aye, little one. We be the richest pirates on the seven seas."

"Aye, Cap'N."

So, while in route to Dragons' Island the *Dark Lady* came upon a cruise ship and a mighty cruise ship she was, they came along side the huge vessel as she drifted in the ocean.

"Ahoy mates! We be partakin' this ship and grabbin' all the booty we can carry or throw overboard."

"Aye, Cap'N."

"Yer be needin' to climb that ther' mast and rope the side of that ther' vessel to get on board. Well, what ye waitin' for ye mangy cockroaches?"

And one after another each of the mates climbed the three masts and tossed a rope to the side of the ship. Each one climbed like they had never climbed before until they reached the top where they stopped and looked down from where they came.

Red-Eye Jack roared, “Keep movin’ ye yellow bellied scallywags.”

Finally after they were all on board they joined together in a group and commenced walking the ship.

“A good afternoon to all ye fine landlubbers. Me and me men be here to entertain you.”

The crew shouted a loud, “Aye, Cap’N Bo.”

“This be me first mate Red-Eye Jack and he be one of the toughest swabs aboard me ship.”

The Captain drew his sword and said to the growing crowd, “Look at me new sword. She be a real beauty made of the finest steel and she be slashin’ the biggest of men.”

Another loud cry came from the crew, “Aye Cap’N,” as they pulled their swords and daggers.

Red-Eye Jack raised his sword and announced, “We be takin’ yer booty now ye lily-livered landlubbers. Smartly there, pirates,” as they quickly gathered the treasures going from deck to deck until they couldn’t carry anymore.

By the time the pirates made their rounds the Captain of the cruise ship was summoned who couldn’t believe what he was hearing. After gathering enough men to locate the pirates, it was too late. Captain Bo and his men already left the ship and shimmied down their hearty ropes back on board the *Dark Lady*.

“Hoist them sails mates, we be departin,’” ordered the Captain.

Catching the wind with the tips of her sails she slowly pulled away from the massive ship moving at around ten knots and then all at once she vanished.

Unbeknownst to the crew Midnight and his Ghost

Riders watched from high above the Atlantic Ocean as the pirates continued their trek across the open sea.

Roedee was so full of himself. He had never even heard of pirates until coming across Captain Bo, and he yearned to be sailing right along with him.

"*Roedee, you can't be a pirate,*" ordered Midnight. "*Your job is to fight evil and these men are evil. They cheat and steal and rob the rich and poor.*"

Ghost Kitty asked, "*What makes you want to be a pirate anyway Roedee.*"

The little mouse lowered his head and said, "*Awl, you guys just wouldn't understand,*" and nothing else was said about the matter.

The trio returned to the great pyramids where they tried to come up with a plan to get the pirates to stop their evil ways. *Dragon* and the *gargyies* were always nearby. They thought and came up with a plan.

"*Dragon, you and the gargyies meet us at Dragon's Island. We've got work to do,*" appealed Midnight.

"Arrr, we be seein' yar thar' matey," shouted the *dragon.*

"*Oh, man, not you too,*" said Ghost Kitty. "*We're supposed to be superheroes, not pirates,*" and they disappeared.

Dragon's Island was off the northeast coast of New Zealand's Barrier Island, and it took the crew many months to cross the open waters from the Atlantic to the Pacific. But it was worth the trip. It was a pirate's haven where sea thieves and outlaws gathered and where a hostile crew could shiver their timbers. Surrounded by calm seas, it was partly a barren island with palm trees swaying in the breeze and dry open grassland next to a tropical forest.

The island was true to her name as it was populated by the Komodo dragon. Giant lizards with tails as long as their bodies, with some being up to thirty feet long and weighing over three hundred pounds with brick red skin. Sixty serrated teeth that were frequently replaced, as they devoured their prey using their powerful forearms and claws, and a long yellow forked tongue with a bite so toxic it could leave you dead in a matter of days.

When Lady Grace came on shore Captain Bo took her by the arm and said, “Ye be warned lass of the dragons.”

He turned to his men and said, “Avast, me hearties. Look lively there if yer bones have any value. This ‘er island tain’t much for fools.”

And off they went passing over the dry grasslands into the tropical forest. Using their machetes they forged a path for the Captain to follow.

Red-Eye Jack stopped and snarled, “Ye swabs, yer furgot the grog ye sorry lookin’ sea monkies.”

So, half the crew returned to the ship with Red-Eye Jack and the other half searched for shelter leaving Lady Grace and the Captain alone in the forest. She tried to wear a brave face when she saw her first dragon, but she was more than scared, she was petrified and couldn’t move. Captain Bo faced away from her as the dragon came closer. She started to sweat. Drops of water ran down her cheeks. She swallowed hard and was terrified the dragon would notice her and he did, as he came within a few feet of her timid body.

“Cap’N,” she whispered but it was too late. The dragon took hold of her lower right leg as she fell to the ground.

She screamed, "Cap'N, me be takin' down by tha' dragon."

He turned and drew his sword and fought the giant beast until it released her leg. He drew his pistol and fired and the dragon lay dead beside her.

She was bleeding badly from the deep bites and it would only be a matter of days before the toxins would take effect. He tore off part of his coat to make a bandage and packed her wounds stopping the bleeding. He had no antidote and the Captain was fearful of losing the wench.

They made camp and several days passed as she grew more and more faint. The toxins had made their way into her blood stream, and it wouldn't be long before she succumbed to the bite of the dragon.

The trio had been on the island ever since the pirates came on shore and they watched from afar waiting for the right moment to appear and the moment had come as Lady Grace grew closer to death. The Captain was troubled. He had never lost a crew member before and especially not one as lovely as the Lady Grace.

"Okay, Roedee, now's your chance to become a pirate," proclaimed Midnight. *"In fact, we all have to become pirates and join the crew until we can convince them to change their evil ways."*

And then much to their surprise Midnight shouted, *"What say ye scallywags?"*

Ghost Kitty shook his head and replied, *"Me guess me be a pirate, Arrr."*

Roedee was so excited. He jumped up and cried, *"Arrr, now that's what I be talkin' about mates."*

So, they made their grand entrance next to the burning fire. Red-Eye Jack was first to notice and surmised they were evil spirits from Davy Jones locker as he saw them appear out of thin air.

"Yargh, Cap'N, ye be lookin' at them critters by the fire. They be strange bully boys."

All at once they vanished and reappeared next to Lady Grace placing their paws upon her as the collars around their necks started to glow. The pirates saw the wound on her leg heal in front of their very eyes and her fever break as she awakened without any signs of infection. After witnessing such a masterful feat Captain Bo started to shed a tear, which he quickly hid from his crew.

"She be healed. What kind of critters be ye?" he asked.

Red-Eye Jack was swift to answer. "They be evil spirits from Davy Jones locker."

This produced great fear among the men thinking the trio carried the souls of drowned pirates. Midnight was first to speak.

"Ye be watchin' yer step Cap'N. We be more than just spirits of drowned pirates. We be wantin' to join yer crew. What say ye Cap'N?"

His eyes opened wide as he heard the black cat speak but he stood silent not sure of what he heard.

Ghost Kitty strolled up next to Red-Eye Jack and stared him square in the eye and sent him a telepathic message, *"Ye best be believin' what yer seein' and stop ye whinin' ye mangy dawg."*

Looking around wondering if anyone else heard what he heard he said, "Shiver me timbers Cap'N, what say ye?"

At that moment Roedee appeared in the Captains hat,

running back and forth compelling him to remove his hat and stare at the little mouse.

"Ahoy mates," shouted Captain Bo.

Roedee responded, *"Ahoy Cap'N, we be takin' yer booty and leave yer marooned on this here island. What say ye?"*

Well, of course the mighty man laughed as did his crew. Lady Grace placed Roedee in the palm of her hand and let it be known, "These swine's be healin' me Cap'N and yer not forget."

"Yargh, wench, me not forget."

He looked at his crew and said, "They be honorary pirates, mates and ye be as loyal to them as yer been loyal to me."

A loud, "Aye, Cap'N" followed.

The Captain's parrot, *Sea Dog* stood steadfast on his shoulder and balked, "Me be the Cap'N's favorite, me be the Cap'N's favorite."

Roedee couldn't resist as he appeared beside the parrot on the Captains shoulder and asked, *"Ye be talkin' to me bird? Ye be talkin' to me?"* and the bird flew away leaving behind a piece of his red and blue tail feathers.

"Avast," yelled the Captain as he took the little mouse and placed a miniature pirate hat on his head and placed the pieces of feathers in the rim.

"Yargh, ye be a true pirate now mate," and everyone took part in sharing the rum.

"Arrr, this be good grog," shouted the mates and they drank and drank until they all had fallen asleep.

As the sun rose the next morning Captain Bo was first to rise. He looked around and saw his crew still passed out from the night before and bellowed, "Get up and show a leg, it be dawn ye scurvy swabs."

Weary from a nighttime of celebrating they moaned and groaned as they came to their feet followed by loud yawns, smacking of their lips and scratching of their bellies.

"We be needin' mer sleep Cap'N," muttered one mate as he closed his eyes.

"Yer been dreamin' of wenches all night Arrr…will you bilge pirate?" he asked as he placed his sword to the neck of his mate.

"Aye, Cap'N, Aye."

The trio appeared next to Red-Eye Jack who said, "Shiver me timbers, what might ye be wantin' with the likes of me, Arrr?"

Roedee wearing his miniature pirate hat and small patch over one eye said, *"Avast matey, we be boardin' the Dark Lady and raise the Jolly Roger, savvy?"*

Ghost Kitty wearing a sash across his chest snarled, *"Before the sun strikes the yardarm we be sailin' mates or yer be landlocked."*

Midnight wearing a bandana with skull bones shouted, *"We be sailin' out for six bulge rat infested days, what say ye Cap'N?"*

Looking somewhat swaggered Captain Bo roared, "We be sailin' mates. Blast those pox faced scow slaves larkin' about. We not be landlocked."

And off they drifted gliding along in the calm waters at six knots. After three days at sea they came upon an uncharted island and off the tip of the island was wreckage of a ship, a small yacht that had a hole in her starboard. The people on board were marooned and in much need of help. Captain Bo was not at all interested in lending a hand as this was a ship he'd already captured and it had nothing more to offer him.

Midnight warned the Captain, *"Yar be helpin' them landlubbers that yar 'ave harmed or yer be payin' tha' price."*

Captain Bo responded, "Yer be lackin' pirratude Cat. Only pirates be allowed in this here place of plunder. We not be helpin' 'em blighted landlubbers."

All at once the sky grew dark as clouds filled with rain and blocked the sun. The thunder roared as lightning bolted overhead striking close to the *Dark Lady*. The swells rose higher and higher as the storm brewed.

"Ahoy mates, keep the keel side down, it be clear just o'er the horizon," shouted the Captain.

The crew lowered the sails as the first mate tried to hold her steady at the helm. The motion of the waves was making Ghost Kitty sea-sick as he turned a shade of green.

"Midnight, help me I just can't hang on. This is way too hard," begged the forlorn cat.

The trio vanished off the ship to a safe distance where they watched from afar. At that moment the *dragon* appeared in the rushing water next to the pirate ship. Spitting fire on each side of the vessel the *dragon* spread his wings and lingered over the main mast using his huge claws to hold tight as he lifted her out of the water and dropped her back into the sea.

The *gargyies* stormed the deck nipping and biting the haggard sailors. The waters again turned calm and the trio came back on board. Midnight warned the Captain again.

"Yar be helpin' them landlubbers that yar 'ave harmed or ye be payin' tha' price. What say ye Cap'N?"

"Grab the cockboat mates and go ashore and rescue them yellow bellied landlubbers. We then be settin' sail."

The sound of the crew resonated around the deck, "Aye, Cap'N."

Once the marooned crew was on board the Captain ordered, "Ahoy mates, hoist them sails and let the wind be at ye stern."

He looked at Midnight and asked, "Arrr, tell me what me plans be now *Cat*."

With great pirratude the black cat meowed, *"Avast me hearties, ye an these scurvy scallywags be takin' these lubbers to safety, savvy?"*

"Savvy," answered Captain Bo.

Ghost Kitty was still feeling a bit under the weather as the *Dark Lady* reached ten knots. He was having second thoughts about being a superhero and being mortal. He developed quite an *"all about me"* attitude.

"Midnight, I don't know about all this superhero stuff anymore. I mean, what's in it for me?"

With anger the black cat spit and released his claws from their protective sheaths and said, *"You're a Ghost Rider and you made the commitment to protect the innocents. Now get over yourself and do your job."*

"But, it's too hard and we could die."

"You can't quit, or. . . ."

"Or what?" growled the suddenly brave white cat.

Nothing further was said as the two parted and sulked on opposite ends of the ship. After three more days at sea the castaways who were once marooned were taken ashore and that which had been stolen from them was returned at the insistence of the *Ghost Riders*.

Meanwhile Roedee who was perched high up in the crows nest noticed a Coast Guard ship approaching at a fast speed.

"*Cap'N, we be overtakin' by another vessel;*" he shouted.

"Avast ye bawcocky sea dawgs. Look lively there if yer bones have any value," ordered the Captain.

The cloaking device was engaged and the *Dark Lady* vanished. Midnight appeared next to the first mate Red-Eye Jack who hollered, "Curse that barnacle crusted rotten slab sided tub of sea monkies."

"Hold yer tongues bully boys an let her pass," commanded the Captain.

It was critical that the crew remain quiet as the Coast Guard ship passes as the cloaking device hid only the ship, not the voices of desperate pirates.

Lady Grace while petting Ghost Kitty asked, "How be it yer can speak and do the things ye do?"

He started to respond with pirratude which he had thought all along was ridiculous but then he fluttered his dark blue eyes at the beautiful wench and said with great sincerity, "*We have special powers and we are here to help you and these so-called pirates do the right thing.*"

This was the first time she realized that the fun and games of being a pirate were really hurting people but she didn't want to give it up, so she asked, "Might thar' be another way matey?"

The Captain walked up behind her and demanded,

"Arrr, what might ye be talkin' about behind me back lass?" Lady Grace knew the Captain was very much in love with her and she believed he would do anything she asked.

"Me be makin' a plan Cap'N to save the *Dark Lady*."

"Yargh, well blow me down lass. Just wha' might yer be thinkin'?"

She said with the greatest of confidence, "Me be thinkin' the *Dark Lady* be landlocked."

He was so shocked by her suggestion that he ordered the crew swabbing the deck, "Belay the swabbin' ya mangy cockroaches and take this wench to the bilge."

This was the order Red-Eye Jack had been waiting for. He never believed wenches should be on board a ship anyway, because they bring nothing but bad luck.

He said, "Aye, Cap'N, me be takin' the wench an put her in leg irons." As he walked away with the frightened young woman he turned to the Captain and asked, "When might we be makin' er' walk the plank Cap'N?"

But, Captain Bo didn't answer and Lady Grace was escorted below deck.

As darkness fell over the open sea the crew lit lanterns and kept watch as their voyage continued. Ghost Kitty visited the wench in the bilge trying to comfort her but her sadness, crushed her spirit and her heart was heavy.

When morning came the crew was fast asleep as the *Dark Lady* drifted not knowing her latitude and longitude.

"Git yer sorry keesters up or yer be due a floggin' ye good fer nothin' sea rats an be smartly, you swines," barked the Captain.

"Red-Eye Jack, whar might ye be, ye blighted sea dawg?"

With fear the first mate came from below deck and stumbled towards the Captain with a most concerning look on his face. Captain Bo studied him hard as he stood there silent before him.

"Arrr, wha' yer be hidin' fro' me swine?"

Red-Eye Jack continued with his soundless stare so he was asked again, "Avast, wha' yer be hidin' fro' me matey?"

After taking the deepest breath he could, the first mate replied, "Cap'N, Lady Grace, she not be found anywhere on board. What say ye Cap'N?"

That was the wrong question to ask as the Captain, who took his whip and lashed his first mate and ordered all on board to search the *Dark Lady*. After three hours of searching Lady Grace was still missing.

Midnight appeared next to the Captain and tried to explain in language he would understand.

"Cap'N, yer buxom beauty she be held for ransom and ye and yer crew have 'til sundown to change yer evil ways or be caught by the devil whar' ye spend the rest of yer days trapped in Davy Jones locker."

The shipmates cried, "We not be sent to Davy Jones locker Cap'N, yer pay the ransom."

Captain Bo demanded, "Who dare ransom me buxom beauty? This be mutiny I say and all ye swabs be guilty of mutiny an yer walk the plank, ye will."

The trio appeared in the form of a perfect triangle at the bow of the ship as the *dragon* raised up from beneath the fathoms, and the *gargyies* swarmed the deck, nipping and biting the anxious pirates injecting them with empathy juice, all but the Captain.

The collars around the trio's necks started to glow as the sky grew dark. A light showed bright above the ship where Lady Grace could be seen and heard as she besieged, "Cap'N, there be no mutiny. Me ransom is fer ye to agree to landlock the *Dark Lady*."

He couldn't believe what he was seeing or hearing. He shook his head and muttered, "No wench be worth landlockin' the *Dark Lady*. It be against the pirate code."

Roedee appeared in the Captain's festive hat running around forcing the Captain to remove his hat.

"Cap'N, me 'ave a way fer ye to keep yer mates and yer riches an still landlock the Dark Lady."

"Me be listenin' mouse."

Red-Eye Jack approached the Captain from behind causing him to draw his sword and place the steel blade against his neck.

"What business ye got here swine, Arrr?"

Red-Eye Jack was as humble as an innocent child from all the empathy juice when he said, "Aye, Cap'N, yer might be considerin' the little mouse."

So, as they both stood on the quarter deck, Lady Grace appeared before them.

"Arrr, this can't be real mate, shiver me timbers," mumbled Captain Bo as he reached out to touch the lovely wench and realized she was the bona fide Lady Grace.

"What say ye Cap'N?" she asked as she stared into his dark brown eyes.

"Yer open the *Dark Lady* as an amusement fer the

world to see, an ya earn riches by makin' them swabs pay to git on board. Yer an ye crew kin stay on board puttin' on pirate fights for fun, just like yer did when ye robbed them sea voyagin' swabs."

She took a step backwards and saluted the Captain and said, "Ye be the most famous swashbuckler tha' world 'ave ever seen. What say ye Cap'N?"

He scratched his scraggly beard and thought for a moment.

Midnight materialized on the helm and told the Captain, "*Ye an yer crew be given a pardon by tha' authorities fer the bad deeds ye 'ave done but ye must put it in writin' an give back all tha' ye 'ave stolen. What say ye, Cap'N?*"

He stood before his men and announced, "We be landlocked an ye all be landlubbers."

When he heard the crews applause, he knew he had made the right decision. Returning to his quarters he sat down and started to write.

"I be draftin' a letter in me finest script on me best parchment askin' fer me pardon."

Lady Grace took her place next to Captain Bo on the quarter deck where the two were married in a most fashionable pirate wedding, with the firing of cannons and all the grog you could drink.

The Jolly Roger flew proudly over the *Dark Lady* as she drifted next to the marina. The crowds came and shared in the fun of being a pirate and Captain Bo, and his crew became the most famous modern day swashbucklers the world had ever known.

The trio looked from afar when Roedee was heard saying, "*Arrr, now that's what I be talkin' about mates.*"

Chapter 26

The trio found themselves in the Great Plains of North America in western South Dakota gazing down upon Black Mountain. The snow capped peaks were surrounded by a sea of green where spruce pines from a distance looked as tall as the mountain. With just a nip of winter in the air this was a beautiful place by day with the clear blue sky accenting the white topped peaks.

But, when nighttime fell this mountain became a place of terror for the people who lived in the town below. This sanctuary with all it's splendor by day became a feeding ground by night where vampirism was a well known practice.

Count Barnabus was leader of the cult and he was well

known by his followers as the son of prophecy. He was a mysterious charismatic man with a magnetic personality, but underneath he was very sinister and where pure evil lurked he reigned.

An occult society who celebrated beneath a crimson moon as the dusk embraced the night. As dawn approached the children of darkness slept. But these weren't your folklore fantasy vampires who drank the blood of the living and left behind corpses. These were a special breed from a gothic culture, an asylum of nocturnal beings that lived as the undead.

They used the blood of animals to represent the replenishment of their vitality and they turned to the moons rays for renewed life. It was obvious that this tribe was of demonic possession.

Only Count Barnabus was capable of changing shape and could become anyone or anything he wanted. He had special powers that helped him control his kingdom. This told the trio he was more than just a humanoid.

"*Midnight,*" whispered Ghost Kitty. "*There's something very familiar about that humanoid.*"

The black cat opened his golden eyes as big as he could and said, "*I feel it too and this whole vampire thing is just a front for something else.*"

"*What do you think Roedee?*" asked his brothers.

With a most serious look and a frown to match, he looked at his brothers and exclaimed, "*It's Zorah!*"

"*Of course, it has to be, but I thought he was destroyed in the triangle with the Shadow People,*" said Ghost Kitty. "*What do we do?*"

Midnight with the greatest degree of certainty said, "*We'll go talk to the professor,*" and they vanished reappearing in New York City where they visited the professor who just happened to be having dinner with a very special lady friend.

The trio made themselves visible only to him but he was so distracted by their presence he became tongue tied.

"Excuse me, umm, but I must make an important phone call."

He left his dinner guest and ventured into the men's room where he was met by the trio.

"Well lads, nice to see you, but you've caught me at a most inopportune moment."

"*Professor, we need your help. It's Zorah.*"

"*Zorah*?" he asked.

"*Yes, he's living in the mountains with quite a gathering of worshipers but we don't think they realize they're under his spell. What can you tell us about vampirism?*"

"Vampirism? In this day and time? How in heavens did he get back in power?"

Roedee stood up on his hind legs and shouted, "*We don't know dude but we're going to make road kill out of that dirtball.*"

Being somewhat caught off guard he asked the trio to meet him back at the lab after he finished dinner and he would do some research.

And long into the early morning the professor studied on the subject and after much review he turned to the trio and explained.

"Lads, from what I've been able to learn about vampirism, they live off the life energy of others. Some are takers and some are victims. From what you've told me, it looks like we are dealing with psychic vampirism in which intimidation, fear, and seduction may be the methods used to pull the person away from their center forcing them to give up their energy to the other. Since *Zorah* is in charge he's much like a dictator who grows more and more powerful while the people suffer. The strong influence the weak. He is most likely draining the energy of his victims directly from their auras."

He continued, "The ritual requires feeding from one person at a time in a secluded place. The animal blood is visualized as glowing red energy and those who act by force will usually get a special rush."

Ghost Kitty asked, *"But how can he control the others to perform these rituals? What's in it for them?"*

"He uses the fulfillment of their fetishes and obsessions which gives them pleasure while feeding. Thus, they are drawn to repeat the process over and over again."

"So, how do we stop him?" asked Midnight.

Rubbing his chin while he pondered he enlightened them with a proposal.

"Lads, you'll have to use your powers of telepathy to block the process. The *gargyies* can assist you by injecting empathy juice into the people in hopes they will turn to a more spiritual source of energy. But, just remember, you are mortals now and you must be very careful."

Their mission, once again was the greatest task they would ever embark, but this time they lived in fear because they were mortal. Should *Zorah* find out he would have the upper hand and he wouldn't stop until he destroyed them all.

"Midnight?" asked Roedee. *"What happens if we get hurt?"*

"We have the power to heal one another, remember? So, we should be okay."

"But, what if we get killed?"

Well then, we have nine lives don't we? Even you Roedee; so be careful and use them wisely."

And that's all that was said about the matter.

They returned to Black Mountain. The darkness of night had fallen over the terrain and torches lit the entryway into a wider opening totally surrounded by rising peaks under a star glittered sky. A fiery inferno blazed as members of the cult danced around the flames making a circle of twenty. Out of the twenty, five fell to the ground and praised Count Barnabus who ordered them to continue with the sacrifice. The familiar smell of sulfur filled the air.

The moon was full and glowed brightly against the darkened sky. The white ball in the heavens was so close to earth you could see the craters that seemed to form the face of a man staring down.

Then each of the five rose to their feet and were handed daggers. They took two steps backwards and each of the five were handed an animal, a bat, a cat, a mouse, a dog and a pig.

They raised their daggers high in the air shouting more praise to Count Barnabus and without warning they plunged the daggers deep into the sides of each animal draining them of all their blood. The dead were then cast into the fire to burn.

Each of the five took the containers holding the blood

and passed it amongst the cult and they drank. Their cruelty and lust gave them pleasure and a feeling of ecstasy. All at once the *gargyies* swarmed around them nipping and biting, injecting them with empathy juice. *Zorah* recognized them immediately and knew the trio was nearby.

Dragon appeared in the northern sky spitting flames on the mountain peaks melting the snow, showering the people with black rain representing their evil ways. Upon seeing the dragon the cult fell to their knees and worshipped Count Barnabus begging him to protect them as they wept in fear.

Of course *Zorah* took this opportunity to drain his victims of all their energy one by one leaving each person unconscious and close to death. The trio appeared in the form of a triangle and cast a light downward and as their collars glowed each of the people awoke and realized they were free from the spell of *Zorah* and they fled never to return again.

Then out of the southern sky the silhouette of a magnificent black cat appeared with the full moon behind her showing off her blood red eyes and silky dark fur. She looked exactly like Midnight except she had powers he didn't possess.

She was thought to be an imp, a lesser demon who serves another demon. A white raven also materialized next to *Zorah* and frightened him so much that he vanished.

The trio grew concerned as they knew nothing about imps or white ravens. The black cat came face to face with Midnight and as her blood red eyes turned gold she spoke, "Do not fear me, I am a *werecat.*"

Roedee could not hold back his question, "*And that means what to me?*"

She glanced his way and her eyes turned red as the little mouse hid behind Ghost Kitty.

The leader of the trio stepped between her and his brothers and asked, "*What strange breed are you werecat?*"

Her eyes turned green as the trio watched not knowing what to expect.

"There are many species of w*erecats* and just like you we have nine lives. We are much like werewolfs but we are felines and being shapeshifters, we can change from one physical form to another, even humans. We are vampire hunters and we hunt evil."

Ghost Kitty asked, "*So, you're after Count Barnabus?*"

"Yes, he has sacrificed many animals and has tortured many humans and he must be stopped."

Roedee came out from behind the big white cat and said, "*So, you're here to join our fight, that's cool.*"

She glanced his way again and growled, "We don't belong to any pride," and she disappeared along with the white raven.

They returned to see the professor who was sound asleep. Ghost Kitty whispered, "*Maybe we should let him sleep and talk to him tomorrow.*"

Roedee sniffed the air with his wet black nose and snapped, "*The way he's sawin' logs, how can anybody sleep?*"

The professor awoke thinking he was dreaming and realized the trio was in need of his help. "Kind of early isn't it lads?" he asked.

"We need to find out about werecats and white ravens?" exclaimed Midnight.

"*Werecats*?" he asked. "There's no such thing as *werecats* or white ravens."

Roedee laughed, *"Yeah, well there's no such thing as animal superheroes but here we are, alive and well."*

The professor smiled, "I see your point Roedee."

He yawned and stretched as he climbed out of bed and stumbled towards the lab. Using all the resources he had available he researched *werecats* and white ravens and said, "Oh, my, this isn't good."

"What professor?" asked the trio.

"Well, ravens are thought to come from the land of spirits. They're highly intelligent and have keen eyesight and hearing. They're strong fliers and they can hover in place or soar the open skies and they've been known to imitate human voice."

Roedee sighed and asked, *"So?"*

Looking at Roedee the professor said, "They eat rodents."

Roedee took a step backwards and shouted, *"Oh, man, I thought I only had to worry about cats and snakes and now you're telling me birds can eat me too?"*

His brothers tried to console him but he wasn't having any of it, because for the very first time in his mortal life, he was scared and losing confidence.

The professor continued. "There's more lads. The raven is known to be an omen of death and so logic tells me, the fact that he is white represents goodness and that may be why *Zorah* fears him and vanished."

The trio stared wondrously. Midnight asked, "*So, what about the werecats?*"

"Well, folklore describes them as being similar to werewolves except they turn into a feline instead of a wolf and not just when the moon is full. They are part spirit and called shapeshifters, which allows them to change their physical form through a metamorphic transformation. They can have two bodies at once and can switch freely between them and death of one can result in death of the other. They are sneaky, whisker twitching manipulators and they are very smart and dangerous. You must be careful lads."

As nighttime fell, the trio was drawn back to Black Mountain where *Zorah* was performing rites of passage ceremonies for the new members of his cult. Still going by the name of Count Barnabus he taught the strong to prey on the weak and drain them of their vital energy.

Along with the animal sacrifices and drinking of their blood the people were convinced they would become immortal so they strived for excellence in the eyes of the Count.

But this clan of vampires actually believed they were blood sucking, neck biting, deviants who fed off one another with silver fangs which magically appeared when the moon was full.

As they took to the city below they maimed and brought their victims close to death and the trio followed behind and healed them just before they reached the point of no return. Each full moon the ritual was repeated and when the moon wasn't full the feeding from animal blood was their only source of energy. They had to be stopped.

The trio tried to use their powers of telepathy to block

the mind control of the Count but they were not successful. The Count had become very strong and powerful.

The *gargyies* were called upon to nip and bite the people injecting them with empathy juice but nothing was working. *Zorah* was in complete control of his people and the trio could only clean up the messes left behind.

The trio returned to the Great Pyramids where they felt safe and received comfort. They called upon the creator.

"Great one, please hear our plea. Being mortal our mystical powers are few and we fear the unknown. Please sanctify us with strength and good judgment so we may protect the innocents. We are weak and powerless against Zorah. We need more power."

A brilliant white light appeared in the darkened sky and from the light they heard the gentle voice of the creator.

"My sons, you have many lessons to learn. You are mortal but you have all the powers you need to defeat the evil one. They are within your reach, seek and you shall find."

And the light grew dim and finally faded away leaving the trio alone in the dark with only a message.

Ghost Kitty, was again having second thoughts about being a superhero. He asked, *"Hey, what am I getting out of all this grief? What's in it for me? I don't know if I want to keep being somebody's punching bag, if you get my drift."*

Roedee wiggled his tail and said, *"Now what's he talkin' about?"*

Midnight with a stern look came nose to nose with the big white cat as each stared into the eyes of the other. With words unspoken they backed off and nothing further was said as they returned to Black Mountain.

Another full moon shines brightly as the tribe of vampires feed on unsuspecting victims. The city streets are dark and damp and behind every shadow lurks a monster that preys on the innocents. *There had to be a way to stop them*, thought Midnight and then he remembered the w*erecats*. He called them by name.

"Werecats show yourselves and help us vanquish the enemy. We need your help. We can't do this alone."

And out of the darkness a group of w*erecats* appeared in all different shapes and sizes with eyes blazing red as they joined the trio to fight the vampires. Then all at once the w*erecats* turned into d*ragoncats* with large dragon like wings, scaly skin and a hairy body of thick fur and they breathed fire. The *gargyies* joined in and nipped and bit each of the evil doers injecting them with empathy juice.

Then d*ragon* appeared in the northern sky and roared as his deep blue eyes turned fiery red. He spit flames surrounding the cult in a ring of fire.

They were frightened and they called upon Count Barnabus to free them but he fled when the white raven appeared.

Roedee hid behind Midnight and Ghost Kitty as the raven looked his way.

"Back off raven, I'm not gonna be your next meal."

The leader of the w*erecats* came near the frightened little mouse and said, "Fear not little one, the white raven is here to protect us all," and then she vanished.

The trio was in much need of rest so they returned to the great pyramids where they regained their strength.

Ghost Kitty after much thought made the announcement, *"I'm leaving the trio and going out on my own. I have too much to lose by staying around here. There's nothing in it for me. I've known what it was like to be immortal and now that we are mortal I just can't function as a superhero. I don't want to know death. I hope you both understand.*"

His brothers were not surprised as they saw it coming, so they said their goodbyes and wished him well on his journey as the great white cat departed.

Roedee asked Midnight, "*We've lost the power of three to make the perfect triangle. What are we going to do?*"

"*We'll be all right Roedee and we'll do just what we have committed to do with or without our brother.*"

It was the time of the new moon and Black Mountain was quiet and peaceful. This was the perfect time for the *Ghost Riders* and the *werecats* to plan their attack against *Zorah*.

Midnight called upon the shapeshifters.

"*Come forth werecats and show yourselves. We have much work to do and we need your help.*"

The white raven appeared perched on the lowest branch of a nearby tree as he introduced the Queen of the *werecats*.

"Jata," he chirped, "celestial star appear before us as the time has come to defeat the wicked."

And out of the blackened sky she appeared.

"We come to serve with you and your brothers," she purred.

"*Well, we're one short thanks to Ghost Kitty chickening out,*" mumbled Roedee.

"*Shush,*" said Midnight as he took his paw and shuffled the little mouse behind him.

"Jata, we need your help to destroy Zorah. Will you help us?" besieged Midnight.

She was joined by the rest of her pride and suddenly there were hundreds and hundreds of *werecats*. Everywhere you looked you could see *werecats* changing into *dragoncats* and back into *werecats* making their numbers look greater than what they really were.

"That'll work," shouted Roedee as he levitated in the air watching them change back and forth. *"How do they do that?"* he asked. "We have many skills little mouse. Watch and you shall learn."

At that moment Midnight realized there was a special place in his heart for Jata. She was beautiful with her long black fur and she was magical and mysterious and he yearned to get to know her better.

"Jata, we must come up with a plan to destroy Zorah but he will not be easily fooled."

They spent hours trying to figure a way to bring down this evil doer as they became better acquainted. She too had feelings for the leader of the *Ghost Riders*.

"Jata, we have tried to defeat Zorah before and he escaped. I don't know how he managed to get away but he did," said Midnight.

"We must use what he desires most in order to lure him into our trap. What might that be?" she purred.

Midnight didn't hesitate with his answer when he said, *"That would be me, the leader of the Ghost Riders."*

Reluctantly she proposed, "Well then, we'll just have to use you for bait."

"Then that means he'll find out I'm mortal."

"Yes, but with our combined powers we can protect you."

With the nod of his head and big golden eyes he acknowledged her suggestion and the plan was put into action. On the night of the next full moon the *werecats* would appear in human form before *Zorah* and his followers, pretending to be part of his clan.

Midnight will show himself and warn *Zorah* to change his evil ways or forever be doomed, at which time the *werecats* will change from their human bodies into *dragoncats* and they will attack as they despise vampires. They will capture *Zorah* before he has a chance to flee by surrounding him with the white raven which he fears. The white raven, also a shapeshifter will reproduce himself a hundred times over. He will bind *Zorah* with chains made of pure silver which will temporarily strip him of his powers as Midnight destroys the evil doer.

The night of the first full moon arrived as *Zorah* and his clan of vampires started their sacrifice of the innocents by draining them of their life energy and blood. *Dragon* and the *gargyies* were nearby.

Midnight appeared before *Zorah* just as planned and said, *"Change your evil ways or forever be doomed."*

With a hearty laugh the leader of the vampires asked, "Where's the rest of your trio cat? Looks like you're all alone."

Roedee appeared and shouted, *"We're here dirtball and we're going to destroy you once and for all."*

Suddenly the *werecats* changed from their human form into *dragoncats* and they attacked the so called protectors of *Zorah* and he was left alone. The white raven appeared in numbers far too many to count and they encircled *Zorah* from the north, south, east and west.

Chains of pure silver were placed upon the evil doer and he was bound and could not escape, at least not for the time being.

Jata positioned herself next to *Zorah* and said, "You are pure evil and you have harmed many animals and humans and you must be destroyed. Our numbers have overtaken you and your clan, you can no longer harm the innocents."

At that moment *Zorah* freed his right arm from the chains of silver and as he raised his sword he thrust it towards Jata killing her by decapitation which is the only way *werecats* can be slain.

Midnight and Roedee took the power of two and cast down a bright light, but their powers were weak, and they could not endure. This moment of weakness cost them dearly.

Zorah burst out of the chains and cast a lightning bolt into the sky striking the leader of the *Ghost Riders* and Midnight fell to the ground in agony as the *Dragon* and the *gargyies* surrounded *Zorah* trying to stop his escape.

Roedee came to the side of his dearest friend and tried to heal him but his energy was drained and his ability to heal was lost and all he could do was watch as his beloved friend breathed his last breath. This was Roedee's first experience with death. He cried, *"My Oolah, my very best-est friend, my Oolah. I'll get you Zorah, you Kitty Wacker. If it's the last thing I ever do, I'll get you."*

The End

Look for the sequel, *Midnight's Ghost Riders*